REDEEMING TRAVIS

KATE WELSH

Steeple
Hill®

Published by Steeple Hill Books™

Special thanks and acknowledgment are given to Kate Welsh for her contribution to the FAITH ON THE LINE series.

This is for the other members of the FAITH ON THE LINE continuity: Gail, Carol, Felicia, Cynthia and Lynn. Thanks for the camaraderie, the cooperation and shared ideas. You certainly all made my book better and lots more fun to write.

Acknowledgments

Brian Krawchuk—ex-air force and favorite nephew. Jeff Sweetin, Special Agent in Charge, U.S. Drug Enforcement Administration, Rocky Mountain Division. Thank you, gentlemen, for your contributions. Any errors found here are mine and certainly not theirs.

STEEPLE HILL BOOKS

Steeple
Hill®

ISBN 0-373-87281-X

REDEEMING TRAVIS

Copyright © 2004 by Steeple Hll Books, Fribourg, Switzerland

www.SteepleHill.com

Printed in U.S.A.

Are not five sparrows sold for two copper coins?
And not one of them is forgotten before God.
—*Luke* 12:6

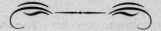

Cast of Characters

Travis Vance—He'd lost everything—his college sweetheart, his young wife and daughter…and his faith. But when his old flame returns, is he ready to risk his heart to her—and the Lord—one more time?

Air Force Major Patricia Streeter—Pretending to be in love with Travis Vance was easy—she'd been there before. But telling her heart that this was just an undercover mission to connect La Mano Oscura and the Diablo crime syndicate was another matter!

El Patrón—Who was the leader of La Mano Oscura that the rogue airmen dealt with?

Maxwell Vance—How involved was Travis's father with La Mano Oscura…and which side was he working for?

Air Force Major Ian Kelly—What secrets did the investigator uncover that left him dead?

Chapter One

From the shadow of an abandoned warehouse Major Patricia Streeter aimed her camera. Through her tele-photo lens she saw the pilot she'd been following hand over an oversize duffel bag to a dark, swarthy man, then take a briefcase in exchange. The transaction took only as long as it took to shoot five quick images of the two men—evidence in her current investigation.

Captain Taylor, one of seven pilots who called them-selves the Buccaneers, opened the briefcase and shook his head, his blond hair glinting in a sliver of sunlight that cut through the alley. "This isn't nearly enough. What are you trying to pull?" she heard him shout.

The second man turned a bit more away from her. Tricia strained to hear him but she could only see him gesture in a way that said "Calm down." Then he shrugged as he said something else that was as equally indiscernible.

"Fine," Taylor snapped. "You're just a messenger. So message this, pal. You tell your boss he'd better get in touch with mine. He has as much, if not more, to lose than the rest of us. It wouldn't be a good thing if people found out he isn't the good guy they all think he is. You tell him this waiting for full payment is making *El Patrón* mighty angry." The taller of the two men by far, Taylor grabbed the other man's jacket. "We're sick of dealing with his threats! We're your boss's bread and butter. He'd be smart to take better care of us. Without the Bucs he has no pipeline, and it takes more than he's giving to keep that pipeline open. *El Patrón* wants a show of faith. A bigger one than this."

The man now in possession of the duffel bag nodded and backed away with another muttered word that scudded through the alley. Patricia snapped a full-frontal picture of this newest subject's dusky face when he turned toward her.

As the conversation played in her mind, she thought, *It was drugs that got you killed, Ian, wasn't it?* Once again Tricia promised her absent friend that she wouldn't rest until his wife and daughters had justice— until *he* had justice. Since the meeting was obviously a drop, she decided to change locations and move back to the street where she could see the license plate on the car the dark-complected man drove. Maybe, if she got lucky, she'd even be able to follow him to his boss.

She pivoted, doubled back around the crates and up the side alley. Hunkering down and watching the ground so she wouldn't trip, Tricia ran swiftly toward the street. And smacked headlong into a wall.

The grunt she heard before the impact sent reverberations down her spine and told her the wall wasn't built of brick, mortar or steel. It was fashioned of all-too-alive flesh and bones. Ready to take down her opponent, she looked up and into the glittering green eyes of the only man she'd ever loved. The man who'd betrayed her by caring more for his needs than hers. The man who'd turned away from her and married her roommate within weeks of her refusing his proposal. She dropped her gaze to his jaw and found it was as rock solid as that annoyingly stubborn chin of his.

Which meant he was furious.

Furious? What did he have to be furious about? And what was he doing there—in the middle of her investigation? "Travis," she hissed, "what are—"

Travis Vance's gaze flicked away toward her quarry, his eyes widening. Then he ground out a low curse, dragged her against him and whirled her around, pressing her back into the cold steel of the warehouse wall. Instantly she became aware of his body heat through her heavy black turtleneck sweater. It disturbed her to be so close to him. Then her vision blurred as his lips descended to hers—lips that were no less furious than the look in his eyes had been.

She grabbed at the fabric of his jacket to shove him away but heard a man's chuckle. "Get a room, amigo," the same man said in a heavy Hispanic accent. Then his footsteps receded, followed by yet another set moving off in the opposite direction. Her pilot was headed back to his car.

Angry at being manhandled, Tricia balled the hand

not gripping his jacket into a fist and drove it into Travis Vance's solar plexis.

"Oomph," he huffed, and stepped back in a hurry, his hand replacing her fist as she shoved him back yet another step.

She stared at him in silence—a silence she couldn't seem to break—her mind having short-circuited the second her gaze locked with his. How could all the feelings she'd thought had long ago faded be so alive and vital after well over a decade?

He wasn't even the same person she'd loved so helplessly in college. In Travis's intense green gaze, where once there had been only vitality and generosity, there was such overwhelming emptiness and bitterness. Oh, his hair still looked as ruffled as ever, but his brow was furrowed from too many years of frowning. Her fingers itched to trace his square jaw and see if that slow grin still pulled his full bottom lip into an expression that could only be described as cocky. But she had an idea his mouth rarely smiled in any way these days and the black hair at his temples was finely threaded with gray. Still, it was clear that time had been kinder to his looks than his soul.

"What did you hit me for?" he asked, still gasping and rubbing his stomach.

It was easy to retrieve her anger. "Don't try to act so amazed or as if you didn't deserve it! What did you think you were doing?" she demanded, flexing her hand behind her back. His six-pack abs were certainly as well developed as ever.

"Did I offend you?" He raised his left eyebrow and his lips did the exact thing she'd wished for moments earlier. That cocky grin emerged from the shadow of the past years. "You've changed, sweet cakes. Time was you'd have thanked me for saving your cute little—"

"Don't say it!" she cut in, silencing what she was sure was a word she'd rather not hear. On top of calling her sweet cakes, she'd probably shoot him. The oaf! The creep! The snake! "Believe me, Travis, I understand that the kiss was nothing but a diversionary tactic. I wasn't born yesterday. I meant, what are you doing *here?*"

His eyes narrowed. "Where exactly is *here?*"

"The middle of my investigation. You just blew my chance for that Hispanic guy's license plate. I'd have known who he is by six tonight if you hadn't gotten in my way. Maybe even where he was headed if I'd had the chance to follow him."

A muscle in his jaw flexed but he maintained his smart-alecky air. "Maybe I just happened along."

Tricia propped her sore hand on her hip. "Why don't I believe you? You almost gave me away."

He smirked. That was the only description that fit his insolent, slightly crooked grin. "I believe it was you who ran into me. You really ought to watch where you were going, Ms. Streeter."

"That's *Major* Streeter, AFOSI. Air Force Office of Special Investigations, in case you don't know. Now answer me," she demanded. "What are you doing here? You followed someone. Which of them was it and why?"

"I'm doing a little legwork on behalf of my brother

and a friend. That's all you need to know. It's a free country. And before you try to dissuade me the way you did Sam, I'll save you the trouble. I don't have a boss to order me off a case I've decided to pursue or to threaten me with suspension."

She knew he was referring to the fact Sam Vance, Travis's younger brother, a Colorado Springs police detective, had been ordered off the investigation into the murder of AFOSI's Major Ian Kelly. Ian's body had been moved clear across Colorado Springs from Peterson Air Force Base and dumped behind the Chapel Hills Mall but AFOSI DNA evidence proved his murder had taken place on the base, so the Air Force had claimed jurisdiction. And Sam Vance had quietly turned over everything he'd already compiled, but he hadn't been happy.

It was an awkward situation for Tricia since she attended the same church as the Vances. But she kept getting mental pictures of Ian laughing with his wife and daughters earlier in the summer at a backyard barbecue. He'd deserved so much more than to be executed for just doing his job. She was going to make whoever killed him pay. And no one, not even the former love of her life, was going to get in her way.

She stepped back and stretched to her full five foot nine inches. "You really don't want to take on the United States Air Force, Travis. AdVance might be an elite name in corporate security and anti-terrorism circles, but compared to the might of the U.S. government, you're small potatoes. And you'll lose. Big-time."

She turned and stalked away. The general was not going to be happy about this when he saw her report. And frankly she couldn't wait to watch the fallout.

Travis watched Patricia stride off. If he'd asked anyone at school to describe her, they'd have said amiable, shy and maybe even a little guarded. He'd found her appealingly mysterious but vulnerable. And what the air of mystery and timidity hadn't done to draw him, her long auburn tresses, short straight nose and wide golden-brown eyes had.

Now he found himself absolutely bowled over by all the changes in her. In his mind, she'd stayed the quiet girl of barely twenty who'd broken his heart. Now he knew she'd gone on—without him. She'd changed so much. She had curves where there'd been none to speak of. Her exceptional hair was now cropped short in what could only be called a nonstyle. But the biggest change of all was that the quiet self-contained young woman he'd known had disappeared and become open, candid about her intentions and nearly volatile. He rubbed his stomach. Maybe *nearly* was a bit too hopeful an adjective. The young woman who'd brought out his every protective instinct was gone and in her place was a warrior in her own right.

Remembering that old Patty and the one personality quirk that had probably foreshadowed all the changes he saw, he listened for the sound of her car. Sure enough, the familiar six-second heavy rev of an engine reached his ears. Ah, the sound of Patty Perturbed. He grinned, wondering if she still drove with the same edgy reck-lessness she'd had in college.

Travis caught himself smiling and scowled. Unfor-tunately, he had a whole lot more to wonder about than her driving. Like if he'd lost his mind when he'd touched her—when that same electric spark he remembered so well from college shot through him once again. Like why matching wits with Patricia Streeter had felt so good.

What was it about her?

In those few moments with her in his arms, he'd felt more alive than he had in years. It was as if that first touch had reawakened all the feelings he'd once had for her. As if all those feelings had been hiding deep inside his frozen heart.

He took a breath and huffed it out in an explosive burst. Why had he been so angry when he'd realized who it was he held in his arms? Could all that latent anger be a sign that he hadn't really gone on with his life when he'd married? Had he been unfaithful to his wife in his heart?

Allison.

Her dark, accusing eyes were burned into his mem-ory. How many times had she charged him with carry-ing his love for Patty so deep inside that he couldn't dislodge it? Had she been right? Believing she'd been wrong was the one thing about their doomed marriage he'd been able to take comfort in.

No! He wouldn't do this to himself. Not again. He *had* come to love Allison and most especially he'd loved their daughter, Natalie. He could still see them as they'd pulled out of the drive that fateful Saturday morning. Identical creamy complexions and raven-black hair, Natalie, so innocently unaware of the tension between her parents. Allison wearing all the tension in her expression that he was trying so hard to hide from their child. Natalie had waved and laughed with excitement and anticipation of a week at her grandparents' house on Lake Henry in New York. Allison hadn't even acknowledged his presence, having refused a ride to the airport.

A week later they'd been gone. A boating accident took all four in a moment's carelessness on the part of a teen taking his friends out for a spin in his father's boat. Travis had envied his in-laws their quick deaths. They'd never known the grief and guilt Travis had.

He didn't even blame the kid who'd been at the helm of the speedboat. Since that day he'd had too many moments of inattention at the wheel of his car, which was potentially just as deadly as that boat had been. The only ones to blame for their deaths were God and himself.

God's failure was obvious. He should have reached out His hand and saved them. That's all it would have taken, and Travis couldn't get past that.

And his own culpability? Just as easy to define.

If he'd been a better husband, Allison would have been at home with Natalie and not on that boat with her parents. The separate vacation had been Allison's way of trying to force him to give up the police force. But he'd been just as determined to remain the person he was. No compromises for Travis Vance. And because he hadn't been willing to consider a change in career, his wife and child had died.

In the long run, when grief, anger and guilt had all but consumed him, the job hadn't been important at all. He'd walked away and hadn't looked back. In fact, AdVance Security and Investigations had grown almost by itself.

His father had asked him to evaluate the security at a friend's company. Plans for a new product had been stolen. The CEO had wanted to find the leak and prevent it from happening again. Travis did both and got hooked on the available technology and ways to prevent corporate espionage.

And the rest was history. AdVance kept him busy three hundred and sixty-five days a year with several regular corporate accounts and a few special assignments interspersed. This favor he was doing for Sam was just such an assignment.

He climbed behind the wheel of his car, forcing himself to think only about the case. A syndicate called Diablo was operating in Colorado Springs and poisoning the town. They were selling street drugs, not the stylish designer drugs of rich and famous vacationers CSPD was used to dealing with. Consequently the city had exploded with a rash of robberies and murders. Drug arrests and drug-related domestic abuse calls were up, as well.

And it looked as if Diablo had ties to the group responsible for the shooting of Dr. Adam Montgomery, Travis's childhood friend. They'd caught the guy directly responsible, but he'd been killed in jail before cracking. Sam had been pulling his hair out before and since and getting nowhere fast. Then a break. An Air Force officer with AFOSI was found murdered. Executed really, his body dumped behind the Chapel Hills Mall. And scribbled on a crumpled piece of paper in his pocket was the name Diablo and La Mano Oscura, the Venezuelan drug cartel Sam thought controlled Diablo.

But then the Air Force had swooped in, claiming jurisdiction, saying Kelly had been killed on base. They'd promised to let the CSPD in on anything they found out about Diablo or its possible ties to La Mano Oscura. But Sam wasn't convinced. If Air Force pilots were involved, who knew if they'd admit it outside military circles? So Travis had offered to "keep his eyes and ears open" but they'd both known what that meant. Travis was on the case.

Travis narrowed his eyes as he put the car in gear and started toward home. Wouldn't Sam have known the name of the Air Force investigator he'd lost the Kelly case to? He had to wonder if he'd been set up by his well-meaning brother. Well, no matter. He'd had to run into Patty Streeter sooner or later. She'd been in town for at least six months now. His mother had made a point to mention several times that Patty was stationed at Peterson Air Force Base and was a member of Good Shepherd Church. He'd seen them all watching for his reaction, too. He was proud to say that reaction had been negligible. Patty, or as his mother referred to her, Tricia, was in his past.

He chuckled mirthlessly as he turned onto Platte Avenue on his way home to Manitou Springs. Until a few minutes ago he'd actually believed that rubbish.

Chapter Two

Tricia watched in stunned silence early the next morning as Travis's father, Maxwell Vance, pillar of Good Shepherd Church, approached General Hadley. Today she'd been tailing the general but had thought this trip across town to the Air Force Academy would be routine. Apparently it was anything but routine.

The two men stood talking on the top step outside the cadet chapel. Hadley, short and stocky, reminded Tricia of a nasty bulldog. He was dwarfed by Max Vance, who was almost as tall and rangy as his son. Their conversation seemed amiable and without purpose at first.

Did this mean she was wrong in suspecting the general? Or was the father Travis had so idolized back when they'd known each other mixed up with Diablo, drugs and murder? She knew firsthand that parents could be less than perfect. Tricia also knew they could be on the wrong side of the law. Hers had been.

The thoughts floating through her mind made her shiver in the cool October breeze but it was really the idea of a sinister meeting taking place at the chapel that chilled her to the bone, especially when the atmosphere between the two men changed. As she watched through her telephoto lens, Tricia snapped a shot of the general as he shook his head and stepped back from the other man, looking nervous and as if he were suppressing an angry reaction. Maxwell Vance's attitude seemed too amiable to have caused such a reaction in Hadley. Especially considering what she knew about the general's reputation for being cantankerous and gruff.

Why was he hiding his anger and why the nervousness? Even more at odds with his reaction was the fact that, though Vance was an upstanding member of the community, he should be no threat to Hadley.

Then Travis's father said something else and walked away with a shrug. He sauntered to his car as if he didn't have a care in the world, flipping his keys around his index finger just as Travis always had. She followed his progress, snapping a few shots till he climbed behind the wheel of his silver Mercedes and left the area. He seemed cool and unaffected by the meeting, but when she scanned back to the top step, she found Hadley still staring after Vance, looking openly tense now. His anger was no longer disguised, either.

She reminded herself the meeting could mean nothing but found herself worried anyway. Max Vance had seemed so very deliberate in the way he'd approached Hadley. Was this encounter linked to Captain Taylor's displeasure at the drop yesterday? Taylor had demanded the swarthy man's boss get in touch with his. Officially,

General Hadley was Taylor's boss. Could he be Taylor's boss in this illegal business, as well? Could Maxwell Vance be the man her Hispanic bag carrier answered to? Had Vance come there in answer to the general's demand? If so, he'd told the general something he didn't like hearing.

Her heart suddenly heavy, Tricia felt as if her own hero was teetering on the brink, ready to fall off his pedestal instead of Travis's. She wanted to reject the notion out of hand but couldn't because it could endanger the lives of his sons, daughter and wife. She pursed her lips. Whatever the truth was, she had to find it. She sighed. This was just one more reason to find all the Diablo connections on the base and help rid the community of a growing menace.

She lowered the camera and checked her watch. Time to report in with General Fielding. It wasn't a meeting she looked forward to, but she couldn't keep a three-star general waiting. Not even with information guaranteed to make him hit the roof over the culpability of Air Force personnel and all the civilian interference she'd run into thus far.

Tricia went back to her office and did a quick and dirty search of Maxwell Vance's military records. It netted her lots of questions and absolutely no answers. Vance had spent decades in the Army yet he'd retired a lowly sergeant. His family lived too well for his pay grade and they'd never lived at a duty station with him. Max Vance didn't add up at all.

Two hours later, whether she was ready or not, she

walked in and saluted Lieutenant General Charles Fielding standing at attention in front of his desk.

The general kept his nicely appointed office free of all clutter so that the highly polished mahogany desk and bookshelves gleamed in the sunshine that poured in through the windows behind him. Photographs of his late wife and grown son were dotted throughout the room between an odd assortment of mementos. The room somehow managed to look homey and business-like at once.

"At ease, and be seated, Major," he said. "And tell me something I want to hear."

General Fielding was a tall man in his very early sixties who'd given up on hair when it had given up on him. He simply shaved it all off the same way he shaved his youthful face. His most memorable feature was blue eyes that had all the cutting power of a laser when he aimed them at a junior officer. She felt that heat now as she settled into the leather chair in front of his desk.

Tricia swallowed. "I'm sorry, sir. The autopsy report on Ian…uh…Major Kelly showed exactly what the prelim did. He was forced to his knees and shot in the back of the head at point-blank range. His body was moved off base, I would imagine in the hope of throwing suspicion out into the community. The medical examiner turned up no other useful evidence. But Luminol and DNA tests show Major Kelly was killed on the flight line, in hangar four. Sir, there's a killer somewhere on base with blood not only on his hands but on his uniform, as well."

"Unless he or she managed to dispose of it when they got rid of the body. It's Hadley or one of his pilots, right?"

"I'd say so, sir."

"The Air Force went to a lot of trouble to move Hadley and his wing here where they could be watched. We aren't in the habit of temporarily shutting down bases, even one as small as Cascade."

"That story about a geological survey showing a major fault line running under Cascade was brilliant, sir."

Rather than smile at the comment, the general frowned. "Yes it was, Major. And this idea apparently cost Major Kelly his life. Are you closer to proving who killed him?"

Tricia hesitated. She knew General Fielding felt terribly responsible for Ian's death, though he'd never say so. "Not yet, sir. But on that front, I tailed Captain Taylor from the Meadow Lake Airport where the Buccaneers keep their F-100 Super Sabre. Taylor went straight to the general after reporting in at the flight line. He left twenty minutes later, however. The general's secretary wasn't on duty during that time so he may not be involved. General Hadley's office door and his desk line up with the outer office door and the approaching hall. The general left both doors open so I'd have been seen if I'd tried to get close enough to hear what was being said. Money was the subject, though. I heard Captain Taylor say something about it. Even though I don't know the context, it ties in with something I heard later."

She caught the glitter in General Fielding's eyes before she continued. "Taylor left the general and went immediately to the warehouses close to the Colorado Springs airport. There he met with a swarthy man and exchanged the duffel bag for a briefcase. I got a few black-and-white shots of the meeting and the exchange. They appeared to argue, but I couldn't hear all of what was said. I *was* able to hear Taylor demand more money then tell the subject to give a message to his boss to contact—" She hesitated. "I'd have to say he meant General Hadley, sir, but he didn't use his name. Right after that I ran into trouble."

General Fielding shot her his infamous scowl. "What happened?"

"Do you recall the police detective who originally had Major Kelly's murder case?"

He narrowed his eyes slightly in thought. Charles Fielding truly had a mind like a steel trap. "Vance. He seemed annoyed but he was cooperative."

"Yes. That would be *Sam*. His older brother—*Travis* Vance—is the trouble I ran into. He's an ex-cop turned corporate counterespionage, counterterrorism expert. He caused me to miss the chance to follow the new subject and the bag. Nor did I get a positive ID on the subject because of him."

Hoping the general wouldn't want to go into what happened further, she flipped open her notebook and went over the chronology again. "I can tell you Captain Taylor landed at Meadow Lake at 1730, checked in at the flight line at 1800, met with General Hadley at 1845. He then went to the meeting behind the warehouse at approximately 1900 and immediately passed on the bag that he'd kept with him since he landed. That was when I heard money spoken of again."

The scowl on the general's face grew more pronounced when he slapped his desk. "It has to be drugs. I want these men, Major. Your promotion is riding on how fast I get them. Tell me how this Travis Vance stopped you from following up on the subject and where that bag was headed."

Tricia felt her face heat and made sure her response didn't sound too familiar. "Vance is not a small man, sir. And I gathered we were spotted when I ran into him."

"*Ran into?* Literally?"

She fought the urge to grimace. "Yes, sir. That's why he had to create a diversion, so we wouldn't be recognized, but that meant I couldn't follow the subject."

"And what exactly did Vance do to create this diversion?"

Tricia gritted her teeth. She'd kill Travis for this. "He kissed me, sir. It…ah…managed to hide our identities nicely. Actually, it worked out quite well because I was able to hear the unidentified subject's voice. From that little snippet of conversation, I'm pretty sure I was able to determine his ethnic background and social placement."

"And that is?"

"Hispanic, and I would say at best, lower middle class."

"And what did he say to help you determine all that in—what did you call it—a snippet?"

Tricia squirmed a bit in her seat. "He called Mr.

Vance 'amigo' and he spoke in accented English. And—" She hesitated but the general motioned with his hand for her to continue. "He told Travis to get a room, sir. Hardly the comment of a gentleman."

General Fielding coughed. "I see," he said at last. It looked to her as if he was actually fighting a grin, but she wouldn't have sworn to it. Charles Fielding was a real hard-liner so a grin during an interview would be a first, she was sure. What she was also sure of was that the three-star general on the other side of the desk didn't *see* half of the effect that kiss had had on her and she sincerely thanked God he didn't.

It was Tricia's turn to clear her throat before she went on with her explanation. "As soon as both subjects were out of our hearing, I demanded to know what Travis was doing stumbling around in the middle of my investigation. He made reference to legwork for his brother and a friend. Later, I remembered who that friend probably is. Dr. Adam Montgomery is a member of my church. He was working in Venezuela at a clinic when he interrupted a robbery and was shot. He was flown back here for treatment."

"I remember that story in the news this summer. It was another doctor who shot him. And he made a second attempt here in Colorado Springs. Right?"

She nodded. "A Dr. Valenti turned out to be the perp. And it was more than one more attempt here. But he was killed in the jail by—" she checked her notes"—an inmate named Jorge Jaramillo. Detective Vance saw the note the crime scene investigators found in Major Kelly's pocket as the break he needed in his investigation of the Diablo problem here in the city."

"So he involved his brother rather than make official waves?" the general asked.

"It could be that this is Travis Vance's idea. Adam Montgomery has been a close friend since childhood. Sir, I don't see us dissuading him. He's as stubborn as the day is long. And there's something else."

The general frowned. "Something else? Major, you aren't making me a happy man."

Sighing, Tricia said, "I know that, sir. And I apologize for disappointing you. A little while ago I was tailing General Hadley. He met with *Maxwell* Vance at the academy."

"Another brother?"

She shook her head. "Their father. It could have been innocent but…well, sir, I'm concerned. The general seemed agitated. Mr. Vance was cool and calm."

"What is your take on General Hadley?"

"I don't think he's a stupid man," she said, not wanting to condemn a senior officer without proof. "And he seems to meet excessively with the Buccaneers…that is with most of the seven pilots who co-own the F-100."

"It was a lucky break Captain Johnston was more loyal to the Air Force than the other Buccaneers and decided to approach Major Kelly. I shudder to think how long this might have gone on with no one the wiser."

"Ian—Major Kelly—logged several flights for each of the Buccaneers in the past four months since they transferred here. And Captain Taylor took the duffel bag with him off the flight line to the general's office, though he did leave it locked in his vehicle during their meeting."

"Are you convinced of Hadley's guilt, too? Don't pull punches. You're my eyes and ears out there, Major. I want your opinion."

"He's up to his bull neck, sir."

"Then you get out there and nail him. I want an airtight case. If he killed Ian Kelly, I want a front seat at his execution. What about Maxwell Vance? Is he Hadley's contact with Diablo?"

Once again her training helped Tricia keep from wincing at the thought, but her conscience forced her to add a qualifier. "I couldn't say, sir. He is, however, a respected member of the community as well as my church."

"I seem to remember hearing about a certain nationally known preacher who had his hand in the till not that long ago, so I don't think church attendance proves anything."

"But my church is—"

"Not my concern," General Fielding growled. "Leave your faith in God and in your fellow man at that front gate, Major. You have a job to do and I expect you to do it sans religious blinders. Got it?"

"Yes, sir," she said, acknowledging the order, but at the same time planning ways to share her faith with a man she'd seen as a father figure from their first meeting. He really didn't understand what faith in God could mean.

"Now, what about his sons?" the general said. "If their old man is up to no good, are they? Or would they try to cover for Maxwell Vance if they learned he was?"

Tricia stiffened. "Absolutely not, sir," she said, a little outrage showing on behalf of both brothers.

That arching eyebrow climbed his forehead a notch. "You seem very sure of that. Members of your church again?"

"Detective Vance is, yes. He's a soloist with our praise choir. But he's trying to find out more about Diablo himself. And as far as I know, Travis Vance hasn't darkened the door of a church in ten years. But I do know these two men. They'd never break the law."

"I think you're letting personal issues cloud your judgment. I do, however, see your point about Travis Vance causing problems if he's out there on his own and in the dark about what it is you're up to. And I don't want anyone destroying evidence, so here's what I want you to do…."

Chapter Three

Travis pivoted left, keeping one foot firmly planted then faked back, trying to get away from his attacker. It was a successful move, but his opponent was a cagey, free-thinker from way back. In a blink, he was there blocking Travis's path. His standard five-second window of opportunity was nearly up, so he faked left, then whirled right. He took his shot and buried the opposition.

"Score, little brother. Twenty–sixteen. Age and experience win out once again."

Sam was bent at the waist, sweat soaking his shirt in spite of the cool October temperature. "I'm just out of practice," he huffed. "Too much rich food, I guess."

"I'll remember to thank Jessica," Travis said, grinning as he snatched up two old towels they'd left on a bench near the driveway.

"I'll get you next time, big brother." Sam stood straight and winced as he caught the towel Travis tossed toward him. "Or the time after that. How come you just get harder to beat? You're older. You're supposed to fall apart and this is finally supposed to get easier."

Travis grinned. "In your dreams, bro. So, are you going to pretend you didn't know Patricia Streeter was the Air Force investigator who took over your murder case?"

"Why should I?" Sam asked, apparently a bit amazed by the question. "You've been telling Mom for months Tricia was ancient history. Is there a reason I should have mentioned it?"

For a long moment Travis could only stare at Sam. Caught, he could neither press his brother for his reason for keeping silent nor could he protest the fact that he had. Not without revealing the embarrassing truth that he'd been carrying a secret torch for his ex-girlfriend for years—right through his marriage to Allison.

He shrugged, reaching for nonchalance. "No. I just thought you might have thought to mention it in passing. She hasn't changed much. Still drives like they gave keys to a lunatic let loose from an asylum."

Sam gave Travis a sidelong look. "That's funny. I thought she'd changed a lot. I remembered you bringing home a skinny, long-haired, tomboy who played the guitar."

Travis scowled. "And your point is? Now she's a skinny short-haired tomboy who plays with guns. Not much of an improvement, if you ask me."

"When I had to hand over the case, the chief promised me she's a top-notch investigator. I somehow doubt she was playing when she got that sharpshooter's medal she wears on her dress uniform."

"But then I didn't see her in uniform. Or maybe I did. She had on a black turtleneck and Air Force-blue slacks."

"She's a conservative dresser. She usually attends church in her uniform. She sometimes wears a golf shirt and blue slacks when she volunteers at Galilee Women's Shelter. But Jessi says Tricia stepped back from her volunteer works since taking over the case. I gather Ian Kelly was a special friend of hers."

Travis hated the shaft of jealousy that shot through him. How could he be jealous of a dead man or his relationship with an old girlfriend? He pushed the thought away because it didn't bear thinking about.

"Yeah, well, I'm out of here. There's a shower waiting at home with my name on it. Let's go, Cody," he shouted, and gave a sharp whistle. Bounding out of the backyard came his best friend and almost constant companion. Three-year-old Amy followed, looking a bit forlorn.

Amy was Sam's stepdaughter. Travis and Sam's wife, Jessica, had a lot in common. They'd both lost spouses in accidents, but she'd been luckier. Her daughter had lived. His hand went instinctively to the small gold initial ring he wore on a thick sturdy chain. The ring that lay at the base of his throat had been his third birthday gift to Natalie. He rarely took it off.

It had been hard for Travis to even look at Amy Mathers at first, though the little blonde and his dark-haired daughter, Natalie, looked nothing alike. It was the shy but bright look in her eyes that sharpened his loss into such painful clarity whenever he came in contact with her. Yet like a moth to flame, he was drawn to her just the same.

Amy ran up to him and he found himself instinctively squatting down to her level. "Cody left his ball," she announced.

Sure enough when Travis looked down, clutched in Amy's hand was Cody's slimy, muddy ball. Her dress was no better than the ball from a messy game of doggy catch. "Uh-oh, Mommy's going to have my head for this one," Travis said.

Sam scooped Amy up and the little blonde hugged him around the neck. "You can get dirty all you want. Right, Amy?" he said, his tone so full of love it made Travis's throat ache.

Nodding vigorously Amy added, "Cody can stay?"

Sam shook his head. "He has to go now, but he'll be back."

Amy turned toward Travis, her bottom lip trembling. "Cody can't stay?"

Travis groaned. "Aw, Sam. Get the kid a dog, will you? Every time Cody and I come over I feel guilty leaving with him."

"You want a doggy?" Sam asked the apple of his eye.

Amy's big blue eyes went round as saucers. Her blond ponytail bobbled as she somehow managed to hop up and down while still in Sam's arms. "Can I, Daddy? Can I?"

Sam shot Travis a helpless look.

Travis held up his hand. "Don't even try to put this

one on me. You asked the kid. And let's face it. If she called you Daddy in the same sentence with 'Can I have the moon?' you'd start calling NASA to see if there was a way to get it for her. I'll catch you later, bro. Have fun explaining a puppy to your busy wife," he said, and turned, snapping his fingers for Cody to follow.

"So, Cody, my boy, I'd say it looks as if you're going to have another playmate soon." He, of course, said this loud enough for his dumbfounded brother to hear. Sam was fast learning that fatherhood took practice, and with a three-year-old suddenly bursting into his life, he was going to have to speed up his learning curve…fast.

"Go home," Sam yelled.

Travis turned and saluted his brother with a chuckle, then took off at a jog, dribbling his lucky boyhood basketball down Goldmine Lane. Cody ran ahead then doubled back to run alongside him until some woodland creature got his canine interest and he took off at an energetic run.

Tricia climbed out of her car, tugged her uniform jacket into place and squared her hat. There, she thought, armor in place, she was ready to beard the lion in his den.

Travis must be at home or Sam wouldn't have given her the code when she called and asked for help getting past the gate at the entrance to the gated community. Besides, sitting in the drive were Travis's two questionable vehicles—both she was sure he considered vintage. One of them brought back too many memories so she forced

her gaze away to knock on the door to his pueblo-style
house. No one answered, however. It looked as if all that
mustering of courage would go to waste.

Not one to waste anything, even energy—nervous or
otherwise—she looked around. She was curious about
how Travis lived these days, this man whose life she'd
once thought was too far removed from the one she'd
known. So Tricia stepped back to analyze what she saw,
rather than just leave.

She looked back to the driveway, her eyes drawn to
the dark green 1969 Firebird, and the memories rolled
over her. Glorious ones. The night he almost single-
handedly took the college's basketball team to the state
championships. The day she'd aced the first final in her
major. Then devastating ones. The morning on the way
to school when they learned two friends had been killed
in a car accident. And most especially the night he proposed, when she'd tried to put him off, ending their relationship almost by default.

Tricia shook her head. The past was past. There was
no shame in having made mistakes as long as you made
up for them—or at least tried. She'd hurt Travis by turning him down so clumsily. He'd hurt her by turning to
Allison. Now she was going to make sure he and his
family were protected from his father's folly even if not
exactly on her terms. Thinking of the general's terms,
she turned her mind back to his house. She needed to
size up her opponent.

Travis's deep terra-cotta-colored house looked a bit
forlorn. There was a rock garden that artfully tumbled

away from the walk to the lawn but both lawn and garden were sadly neglected. There were the craftily placed pots scattered on the steps and in the entranceway but those were as empty as the house.

The hollow slapping sound of a bouncing ball and the deep woof of a large dog drew her attention. Tricia turned and looked down the hill in the direction of the noise. It was Travis jogging along the street while he dribbled a basketball. Her heart ached at the sight as she walked back down the drive to meet him. How many times had she seen him like this in her memory… in her dreams?

Reality was different, though, because a huge German shepherd galloped happily along at his side. Travis laughed at the dog's antics but a frown took over his expression the second his gaze fell upon her. He stopped in his tracks at the foot of the drive, the ball falling to the ground and rolling behind him into the street.

The dog immediately trotted to her side and sat, smiling up at her, encouraging affection with his big brown eyes and a raised paw. "I wondered if we could talk," Tricia said to Travis as she automatically stooped to shake the dog's proffered paw. Rather than focus on Travis's thunderous expression, Tricia gave the dog a chance to sniff her hand before petting his soft fur. He very nearly purred.

The dog—not Travis.

Travis was the one who growled, "This is a gated community. How'd you get in?"

"Actually, I called your brother and he gave me the code to the gate."

"I'll have to remember to thank him. I can't imagine that he thought we'd have anything to talk about."

She shrugged, trying for nonchalance as she straightened, her hand resting on the big dog's head. She didn't want Travis to think she wanted this partnership General Fielding had outlined. Though she did indeed want it because it would mean she'd know he was safe. And if she refused to examine that particular reason, using instead the excuse that she liked his mother and worried that his father had put Lidia Vance in danger, then so be it. She could stay up nights worrying and thinking about only so many problems at once.

"I thought you were interested in Diablo. The increase in Colorado Springs's drug problems. La Mano Oscuro," she challenged him.

His eyes widened almost imperceptibly then his frown deepened. "Talk to Sam. They're ultimately his problems," he said, and turned away to retrieve the ball.

The basketball continued to roll down the hill. It got quite a distance with Travis walking after it at a leisurely pace. It had to be a delaying tactic considering that Manitou Springs was built entirely on hills. He would be a year before he caught it at that pace.

Finally, the ball got stuck beneath a parked car. He kicked it free and all the while, Tricia stood her ground in the middle of the driveway, watching his loose-hipped saunter as he came back up the hill. She saw through his act, though. He wasn't as composed as he pretended. Of course, neither was she, but there was every chance he didn't know that.

Travis finally glanced back at the driveway and
looked surprised to see her still standing there. He didn't
know she could no longer be easily scared away. His expression turned thunderous and he confirmed his mood
with his next statement, "You forget how to take subtle
hints? Go away. I do not want to see your face. That too
subtle for you, *Patty?*"

She didn't blink at the name she'd left behind along
with her major insecurities. "I prefer Tricia now. You
should know that if we're going to work together on this."

That slow wiseacre grin replaced the frown on his
craggy features. "Work together? Us? As in you and me?
You've been out in the mountain sun too long, babe."

Even in college before putting up with the Air Force's
own special brand of chauvinism, she'd hated to be
called "babe." "Look, Travis, let's stop dancing around
each other," she snapped. "I've learned some things
you'd give your eye teeth to know. I can save you
months. And you may have information I need. You
want to know who was ultimately responsible for the
shooting of Adam Montgomery. I remember he's an old
friend. I understand that because I want to find the people responsible for Ian Kelly's murder—*my* friend. And
I think we both want to put a stopper in the drug pipeline running into Colorado Springs. Now, invite me in
like a good boy, and we'll learn to share."

"I guess I don't understand why you're so willing to
cooperate with me all of a sudden."

She sighed. "Because General Fielding ordered me
to. He's a little touchy right now about his people nearly

getting killed. And whether you want to admit it or not, you got in my way yesterday and one or both of us could have been killed in that alley."

Travis stared at her, clearly weighing his options. "Fine, but don't get too comfortable. Just because I'm listening, doesn't mean I'm agreeing to anything. I work alone."

He wasn't the only one with options to weigh. If he found out about all of General Fielding's stipulations regarding this joint venture, he'd bolt the door with her on the outside. And no way was she sharing what she suspected without his word that he'd work with her. She had a killer to catch, a drug pipeline to stop and a promotion to win. She couldn't risk him getting in her way again, and the only way to prevent that was to know where he was and what he was up to. And that meant working together—closely.

"You agree to work this with me, or I don't take another step." Then she took a chance that the years had left that basketball-center ego of his intact along with that cocky grin he still had. She set her lips in a challenging smirk of her own and added, "Or are you afraid to work with me?"

His eyebrows climbed, furrowing his forehead even more, then his frown slid into a grin again. A grin she was quickly coming to believe was an artifice to hide his true feelings. Maybe it always had been.

"Me? Afraid of you? Oh, please," he said, his eyes rolling just a bit. "Fine. We'll work the cases together since you seem pretty certain that this is all linked. Besides, I don't want you getting in my way again."

He pivoted lazily and walked up the drive. When he reached the base of the steps, he turned. Neither she nor the dog had moved. And she wouldn't. Not until she got an invitation. Not after that remark. *She* would get in *his* way?

"You coming?" Travis all but snarled.

Tricia wasn't sure which of them he was talking to, her or the dog. But since it looked like the only invitation she was likely to get, she started forward.

The dog shot ahead then toward the front door, the plume of his tail wagging jubilantly. "Traitor," Travis muttered to his canine companion who ran happily past his perturbed master.

It was nice someone was happy with the situation, she thought, and asked, "So, what's your dog's name?"

As she entered an open, tiled foyer, the name "Cody" on Travis's lips barely registered in her brain. Her mind was suddenly ambushed by the flashes of insight the house gave her into his barren life. She could swear her heart actually ached for him.

The rooms before her had wonderful dark wide planked floors that stood out in perfect contrast to the cream color on the rough, adobe-look walls. Unfortunately, that was the only good thing she could say about the two rooms that flowed off the foyer.

She looked around at the emptiness the rooms reflected and wondered how he thought she might make herself too comfortable in such an utterly soulless place. The walls and windows were bare while the living room and dining room areas were lined with card tables. She counted a dozen tables in all and one desk. Strewn with numerous files, each table held folders of a different color. Stacked underneath most of the tables were boxes also filled with the same color files. There was also an industrial-sized shredder in the corner opposite the Spanish-tiled fireplace.

It was, she realized, exactly what it looked like. A disaster of an office with a nod given toward organization. This must be the life center of AdVance Security and Investigations. Which meant he ran the company the way he did everything—alone.

"Oh, my," she said, in control of her thoughts if not her mouth, "I don't think you need to worry that I'll get too comfortable in here." She walked to the first table and picked up a folder. "I've seen jail cells in Third World countries that were more homey than this place."

"Yuk-yuk," he said. "I don't have to please anyone but me. And this pleases me. *And*—" She heard his footsteps moving quickly toward her and, as she whirled to face him, he snatched the folder out of her hand. "I know where everything is." He dropped it back on the table. "Don't touch my stuff. Besides, that's confidential. And don't go getting any ideas about messing with my filing system. I remember how you like to organize. So what's this about information?"

Tricia spotted the kitchen that lay beyond a half wall. It had two counter stools pulled up to a breakfast bar that was set into the half wall between the dining room and the galley kitchen. She walked to the bar, pulled out a chair and sat.

"Why, thank you, Travis. I'd love a nice hot cup of tea. Suppose you tell me what you've learned while you fix it for me."

"I said I'd participate. I didn't say I'd feed you. That comes under the heading of 'too comfortable.'"

"Oh?" She fiddled with a drawing he'd left on the counter. It was done by a small child and showed a tall man and a dog running. Only the dog smiled. Travis and Cody, no doubt about it. She imagined the budding artist was Amy Mathers, his brother Sam's stepdaughter.

"What's 'oh' supposed to mean? Women never say 'oh' in that tone when it doesn't mean a whole lot more."

"It means that I thought the offer of refreshments fell under the heading of civilized." She looked pointedly at the kitchen beyond where he now stood. Wall-to-wall dirty dishes, several empty bread wrappers and three scraped-clean peanut butter jars. It was anything but civilized. "Decorated by Neanderthal Interiors?" she asked, her eyebrows raised.

"I like my kitchen the way it is, too. Come on. We'll talk in the den. It's neat so it won't put your female cleaning hormones into overdrive."

She followed when he gave her no opportunity to protest. "Sit," he ordered when she entered the small room.

His idea of neat and hers were worlds apart. Stack after stack of magazines and newspapers from all over the world took up about a third of the floor space and the end tables and coffee table. There was also a medium-size TV, a wall of bookcases stuffed haphazardly with books, a futon and an old beat-up leather recliner.

The room fit his personality: rumpled, grumpy and brooding.

She chose the futon and, after picking up and stacking several of the newspapers and magazines into a neat pile, she sat in the newly cleared space.

"You're already driving me crazy and we haven't been working together five minutes," he said, raking his hair off his forehead. "So tell me what all you've figured out about Ian Kelly's murder."

"He was killed on the flight line."

"Then it really was about Air Force business." Travis leaned back in his seat. "Sam thought it was something to do with this influx of drugs that are driving him and the rest of CSPD crazy. In that case, I don't see what I can do for you."

She couldn't very well blurt out that his father was looking pretty good as the kingpin of Diablo, the syndicate she thought was the Colorado Springs arm of La Mano Oscura. She was nearly sure the proof of the connection between the two organizations had been within Ian's grasp but couldn't confirm it yet.

"Five or six of our pilots look good for the runners. One of them is the guy I was following yesterday. We can't afford to trip over each other again."

"And how on earth do we explain our being together all the time, or haven't you and your general thought that far?"

Tricia swallowed, and crossed her legs carefully to hide her nervousness. "Well…er…the general has decided on a way to handle it."

Travis raised one eyebrow. "And what is the general's brilliant idea?"

"We're inseparable because—" she tried to make her expression as neutral as she could "—we're dating again."

Chapter Four

"*What* did you say?" Travis bellowed.

And Patricia Streeter, the girl who'd broken his heart and sent his life into a tailspin didn't even blink at his outrage. Instead she sat back, crossed her long legs once again and settled into the soft cushion of the futon.

"I said we're supposed to be dating. We have to act as if we're crazy about each other. You'll go where I go, I'll go where you go. Officially, I'll take leave to give us the time to decide if I want to get out of the Air Force to be with you or if you'll be following me to my next duty station."

"And they say *I'm* crazy," he muttered, and caught himself raking his fingers through his hair again. Why was it he kept blowing his cool with her? She just plain unnerved him. That's all there was to it. He couldn't do it. He just couldn't. To be near her. See her all the time. It wasn't going to happen.

But if he didn't and something happened to her...

Travis had seen the crime scene photos of Major

Kelly. The thought of seeing Patty like that… He shook his head. No, she was Tricia now. *Major Streeter.* That was even better. This woman bore little resemblance to the pretty coed he'd loved to distraction. But it occurred to him that, even with all that had happened and all the years that had passed, none of it mattered. Not in the face of the stark fact that she was searching for the person or persons responsible for Major Kelly's murder, and that by working the case alone she could very well end up as the major had.

He felt himself start to hyperventilate and jumped to his feet to pace across the room then back to his chair. The idea of those men catching her. Of what they might do to her if they did. South American drug cartels were ruthless, and he'd lay odds the guy he'd been tailing the day before was South American. And Sam thought La Mano Oscura could be involved with Diablo. So it stood to reason the Air Force pilots she was after were probably linked to both organizations. It was the only thing that made sense. But proving it? Stopping it? That was another matter.

And why was she so determined?

Jealousy, hot and angry, reared its unreasonable head once again. "You must have been pretty crazy about Kelly to put yourself in this kind of danger to avenge him," he growled. "You really think anyone will believe you're with me only a couple weeks after his death?"

Her lips pressed into a firm line. "Don't try to make more of this than it is. I said Ian was a *friend.* He, his wife and daughters made me feel like one of the family when I was transferred here. They deserve justice. I want the man or men who killed him. So does General Fielding. It's my job and it could mean a promotion for me, too. *Those* are my reasons."

Travis stared at her then nodded, feeling like a prize fool for his anger. They'd been apart for years. He'd had a wife and a child. He pushed away those thoughts. He couldn't think about Allison or Natalie now. He had failed to protect them, but maybe in protecting Tricia he could make up for his failure just a little.

"You like anyone for Kelly's murder?" he asked, pretending a calm he still didn't feel. "The pilot you were tailing, maybe?"

She shrugged. "Maybe." She looked even more troubled. "Maybe someone higher up."

"How high is high?"

"Possibly as high as a brigadier general. George Hadley is his name. We transferred him and his wing to Peterson where they could be watched. They were stationed at Cascade."

Travis remembered reading something about all that a few months back. "The base the Air Force is afraid has a major active fault running under it?"

She smirked. "There's no fault. And no geological survey going on. It's an elaborate ruse to get Hadley and his wing where we can track their movements better. A handful of pilots under him formed a club called the Buccaneers. There are seven members. They bought into a fifties-era F-100 Super Sabre together. They trade weekends taking her up."

Travis narrowed his eyes. This was getting interesting. "That jet has over a thousand-mile range, doesn't it?"

"Sixteen-sixty."

Whistling, Travis grabbed for a notepad so he could take notes. "They could get to a lot of places with it. Tough places to track them to. How'd the Air Force get wise to them in the first place?"

"One of the Bucs reported an odd talk he had with General Hadley. He got the idea Hadley was feeling him out to see if he'd do anything illegal. At the time he thought he was suspected of something. He got indignant and General Hadley accepted his word that he'd done nothing wrong."

"And that was Hadley's misstep?"

"The first we've heard about. Within the following month, the pilot, Captain Kevin Johnston, started to notice some odd things about his fellow Buccaneers. Like more flight hours on the F-100 than those they logged. They all tried to pass it off as hotdogging midflight but they all also seemed to have a bit too much money to spend, considering the cost of those long flights and the loan payments on the plane."

She paused and straightened the magazines, then caught his eyes and stopped, guiltily hiding her hands behind her. Then she cleared her throat and continued. "Then Captain Johnston noticed nearly the same number of miles on each flight the other members took no matter where they claimed to have gone on their time off. He put that together with seeing them looking a little too comfortable around the highest-ranking officer at Cascade, General Hadley. Captain Johnston was in basic with Ian so he came here to Peterson and went to him with his suspicions. Ian took it to Lieutenant General Charles Fielding, the base commander. General Fielding put Ian Kelly on it and Ian suggested the geological survey as an excuse to get them all to Colorado Springs where his presence wouldn't be suspicious and there'd be someone superior to General Hadley. Two months later Ian Kelly was found dead and I was handed the case. I'm trying to nail General Hadley along with the Buccaneers."

"And for that you think you need my help?"

She glared. "What I need is you out of my way, but I know you too well. You as much as said there was no way you were pulling out of this investigation. If I can't intimidate you off the case, I have to ask you to join in on it." She grinned slyly, her eyes wise with knowledge of his character.

It was Travis's turn to glare. He hated that she still knew him so well.

She crossed her legs, drawing his attention momentarily. He'd always loved her long dancer's legs. "I can't intimidate you, can I?" she asked, dragging his attention off her assets and annoying him further.

Not trusting himself to speak, he sent her a wiseacre grin and shook his head.

She grimaced slightly. "Then I guess we're in this together. And that means it's on General Fielding's terms. In that case, it's your turn to tell me what you have so far."

Travis sighed mentally. It looked as if they were part-
ners for the duration. And he had to give her credit—
she'd told him all she seemed to know. "Ramirez is the
name of the guy I was tailing. He's Venezuelan. Which
fits with Sam's theory and, I suppose, Ian Kelly's that
Diablo and La Mano Oscura are linked."

"I didn't find any reference to La Mano Oscura in
his notes but I still think he was working on proof of a
connection."

"But the crime scene investigators found that note in
his pocket when his body was discovered. It had both
Diablo and La Mano Oscura on it. So we knew he must
have thought there was a link."

She nodded. "Ian was the best. He probably got the
evidence and was killed for it."

"So we'll be a little more careful than he was."

"And we'll each have someone to watch our back.
That was more than Ian had. He liked to work alone."

Sensing that she did, too, and hoping to dissuade her
from going off on her own when he wasn't with her,
Travis found himself adding, "And it probably got him
killed."

The day after Travis agreed to work with her, they
planned for Tricia to meet him at the Stagecoach Café.
Since his mother worked there with her old friend
Fiona, Travis dreaded this very public meeting they'd
set up. They were supposed to act as if they had run
into each other only days before—which was quite literally true. The problem was this was to be their first

date, which was supposed to explode into a whirlwind romance—which was a big fat lie. It would never happen.

He wouldn't let it happen.

Tricia didn't seem to mind lying to his family, and had in fact insisted on it. But it wasn't all that easy for him. His mother was going to be sixty-two inches of trouble. The woman had an eye for the lies her children told and always had. He thought he could pull off today, but then to act wildly enamored of Tricia considering their past? Now that was going to be a feat.

Because everything about Tricia just plain annoyed him. From her self-confidence to her uniform, she wasn't the girl he'd loved. The problem was that somehow she was all the more fascinating for the changes he'd seen in her so far.

If he were completely honest with himself, Travis knew he'd have to admit his real problem with the differences was that she had grown and stretched beyond the potential he'd seen in her. She had been right. He would have held her back.

And that really frosted him.

Pulling open the door of the Stagecoach Café, Travis nearly cringed. Both his mother and Fiona were there, as he'd thought they would be. And they'd seen him. It was too late to back out and call off this hoax of a date.

"Travis!" Lidia Vance called out. "Come back here and sit where I can talk to you, while I fold these napkins." She rushed to him, braced her small hands on his forearms and tiptoed from her slight height to peck him on the cheek. Instinctively, Travis wrapped his arms around her small round form and hugged her.

"I can only chat for a few minutes, Mom. I'm meeting someone for lunch. It's a…uh…it's a date."

Travis felt his face heat. This was never going to work. As he expected, his mother was more than mildly surprised. Her eyebrows rose as her big brown eyes widened. "Here? You're bringing a girl here? Is it that nice woman who you met through the auction?"

He almost burst that bubble of hope he'd seen so often in the past and saw again now. She wanted, and he knew even prayed, that he would pick up the pieces of his shattered life. Much as he would like to make his mother happy, he didn't deserve to go on with his life when his wife and child were dead because of his failure as a husband and father. But for now he'd have to let her think her wish was about to come true. Telling her the truth some day in the weeks to come wasn't going to be easy.

Pushing away dark thoughts, Travis explained, "I ran into Patty…uh…Tricia Streeter, I mean. We decided to meet for lunch."

"Tricia?"

He forced a smile he didn't feel, feeling instead like one of the jack-o'-lanterns that were decorating the town. Cardboard. Fake. A sham. "It was good to see her again. I was…surprised how much." That at least was true, much to his disgust.

"That's so nice. You were always such a cute couple," his mother said, patting his arm. There was a mixture of emotions reflected in her dark, almost all-seeing eyes. Principal among them was delight. She'd bought it and Travis watched his last chance for a reprieve vanish with the blooming of his mother's delighted smile.

Chapter Five

"Oh. Here she is now," Lidia Vance exclaimed, beaming a smile at Tricia as she entered the café. "Tricia, it's so good to see you! It seems so long."

Tricia fought the urge to turn tail and run. Travis had obviously told his mother about their lunch date. This was such a bad idea. What had she been thinking? Oh right, she'd decided this was the way to trap Travis into this artificial courtship. Big mistake! Now she was trapped, as well, and she went to church with this woman she was bound to disappoint.

"Lidia, we just spoke at church on Sunday," Tricia said, trying to pretend she hadn't heard the note of delight and hope in the older woman's voice.

Lidia beamed. "But today you're eating with my Travis. Fiona! Come see who's come for lunch with our Travis," she called to her friend, and owner of the Stagecoach Café.

Poor Lidia, once again doomed to disappointment. How could she have forgotten hearing Travis's mother lamenting the life Travis lived when a church member had asked what he was up to these days? Still, thanks to Tricia's suspicions about Max Vance, she really had no choice but to insist Travis keep their ruse a secret from his family.

She fought the urge to roll her eyes at Lidia's effusive greeting when her gaze connected with Travis's. Then she saw that this was harder for him than it was for her and her guilt doubled. Tripled.

"You two come with me," Fiona Montgomery said, menus in her hand as she rushed up to them. She wore a bright smile on her face and an apron tied about her ample waist.

"Well, that about tears it," she heard Travis mutter.

And it did. Now they were well and truly stuck for the duration. The addition of Fiona to the day meant their "romance" would be telegraphed through all branches of the Montgomery and Vance families. Fiona meant no harm but she loved gossip and Western Union had nothing on her for speed or efficiency.

"This must be family day around here," Fiona said, her artificially bright red hair bouncing as she bubbled along the row of tables. "Jake came in a few minutes ago with one of his signature blondes," Fiona went on. "I'm going to clear my special table for you two while the four of you visit for a minute." She shook her head and frowned, laying her hand on Travis's arm and saying in a conspiratorial, low voice, "Try to talk some sense into him. All these women…" She tut-tutted. "It breaks his mother's heart that he won't settle down."

They walked along, passing a few more tables when

Travis stopped next to a well-dressed, sandy-haired man who shared one side of a table with a stylish blonde. The man's blue eyes crinkled at the corners as he shot a crooked grin Travis's way. "You look a little shell-shocked, pal. Forget about the way those two are, did you?" Jake asked, standing and extending his hand to Travis. "I heard your mother's delight at this interesting turn of events all the way back here."

Travis shook his lifelong friend's hand. "I guess I'm out of practice. This is Major Patricia Streeter. Tricia, I've known Jake Montgomery since he was in the playpen tossing his toys at those of us with the freedom of our parents' backyards."

She remembered the stories of Travis's enviable childhood well. "Is this the Jake you got stuck in a tree with when you were ten or so?"

Jake took her hand, his smile utterly charming. She found herself staring into his arresting blue eyes and said, "Pleased to meet you, Jake."

"Well, hello, pretty lady. Did he happen to tell you it was his fault I got stuck up there? He dared me to go higher and I wasn't one to turn down a dare from one of the older kids. It would have meant I was still a baby." He shrugged. "So I climbed higher. And got stuck. Then Travis knew he'd really catch it if he didn't get me down, and he got stuck, too. So we both got punished. His mother made us write 'I will not climb a tree until I'm twelve' twenty-five times."

Travis chuckled. "Twenty-five for you. Fifty for me, because I was older."

Jake never took his eyes off her. It was unnerving. "Where's Travis been hiding you?" he asked, still holding her hand.

Tricia smiled back, not knowing what else to do, and shrugged. He simply made you look at him by his sheer presence. "At Peterson Air Force Base, I guess," she said, unsure how to handle his singular brand of attention. At the moment, with his intense eyes staring into hers, she felt like the only woman in the world. Had it been Travis looking at her like that she'd have melted, but she had no interest in a playboy of this man's caliber.

"Oops. Sorry," Jake said, and pulled his hand back as if he were afraid it would get bitten off. Surprised and wondering if she'd sent out some unconscious signal, she noticed Jake's eyes were all of a sudden on Travis. "I didn't mean to poach on your territory, Trav," Jake added.

Tricia looked quickly toward Travis and was surprised to see his green eyes glittering with what she could only call jealousy. She felt a little thrill but then she realized he was putting on an act and the feeling evaporated like smoke on the wind. She was nothing to Travis Vance but the woman who had ruined his life.

"Just back off, Casanova," Travis grumbled, furthering his pretense of jealousy. "Pay attention to your own date. It's taken me years to find Tricia again."

My, but he was putting on quite a show for the sake of their investigation. He must be more resigned to it than she'd thought. More resigned than even she was now that it had been put into motion. She only wished it was all pretense for both of them. But as much as

Travis had hurt her by turning so quickly—so easily—to Allison, she was still drawn to him and she hated seeing how empty his life had become.

"Not to worry," Jake said, grinning again. "I was just trying to figure out if Lidia and Aunt Fiona were barking up the wrong tree. Glad to see they aren't. You deserve some happiness, Travis. Nice to meet you, Tricia."

"Aren't you going to introduce us, Jake?" a sultry voice asked from behind Jake.

Jake blinked and stepped to the side, then looked down at his pouting companion, clearly having forgotten her. "Oh. Uh...sorry. Cheri Wilson. This is Travis Vance and his friend, Tricia Streeter."

Jake's date wrinkled her nose. "Don't you hate wearing that uniform? It's so unfeminine. So are you a secretary or something like that at the Air Force base, Ms. Streeter?" Cheri's catty tone wasn't lost on either man, Tricia noticed, and neither looked particularly happy at the subtle but out-of-the-blue attack.

Tricia wondered if her response would surprise Travis. It would if he didn't realize yet how much she'd changed. In college she would have backed down and let the prettier, richer, smarter girl win the encounter by default. But the new Tricia stuck up for herself. "That's *Major* Streeter and I'm an investigator with the Air Force Office of Special Investigation. Travis, I think Fiona has that table ready. Perhaps we should leave Jake and Cheri to their meal. It was wonderful meeting such an old friend of Travis's, Jake. Perhaps we'll run into each other again."

She heard Travis mutter, "Not if I have anything to say about it, you won't." For a split second, Tricia felt another little thrill but then Jake laughed, having heard, as well, and she was again sure Travis's jealousy was all part of an act.

After Fiona seated them and took drink orders, she bustled off and Tricia cautioned, "I thought this was just supposed to be our first date. Your reaction to Jake was a little bit of overkill, though I commend your acting ability."

"Well, I don't commend yours," he snapped. "What was all that starstruck staring into his eyes supposed to be about? The premise is that you're here with *me,* beginning a wild romance, remember?"

Tricia refused to rise to the bait. She was good at her job and she wouldn't let him undermine her confidence in herself or in her ability to do whatever was necessary to get her job done. "I have a job to do but I'm not dead. Jake's a very attractive man. Tell me more about him."

"He's dangerous to women and he doesn't even know it. *That's* what makes him so dangerous. Women from two to ninety-two fall under his spell with no effort on his part. He's left a trail of broken hearts starting from grade school, through high school and college right up to Cheri over there."

"She looked pretty happy to me. Not very nice but pleased with herself as we moved away."

"But what she doesn't know is that she just overstepped the invisible boundaries of one of his relationships."

Fiona came up and dropped off their drinks. "Are you

two ready to eat? If not, I can come back later. I don't want to intrude."

Travis smiled indulgently and shook his head. "Let's just let Mom feed us. She knows what I like and Tricia spent a few weekends at our house when we knew each other before. Mom never forgets anyone's eating habits."

"Okeedokee," she said, scribbling on her order pad and flitting away.

"She's a real character," Tricia said.

Grinning Travis nodded. "Yeah, a real menace. Uh-oh. Looks like Cheri just flounced out ahead of Jake. Another one bites the dust."

"So her jealous act really did earn her the boot. What does Jake do for a living, by the way?"

"He's with the FBI. A computer expert."

"Hmm. Maybe at some point we'll be able to tap him as a resource."

Travis pursed his lips and nodded, thinking deeply for a long moment before saying, "Yeah, maybe. I have in the past. When I first got into corporate espionage I needed to learn about computers and Jake taught me a lot. He's a whiz."

"If we need to call in a whiz then we'll know who to call."

Lidia bustled up with a tray laden with Italian delights. "I remembered how much you liked my manicotti and *braciole* when you visited. Made fresh this morning. Here you go, dear."

"Thanks, Lidia. I can't believe you remembered that after all these years."

"A mother never forgets."

"I thought that was 'A Vance never forgets,'" Travis teased, then looked down at his plate as Lidia set it in front of him.

Travis stared down at his plate. "Mom, why did I get a salad? It looks great but I get the feeling you just put me on a diet. You trying to tell me something?"

"I'm tellin' you that I know you don't eat healthy. Peanut-butter sandwiches for dinner. Disgraceful. Now eat your vegetables," Lidia ordered, then rushed away.

"Sam's a dead man," Travis growled.

Tricia laughed. She'd always loved the byplay between the Vance siblings.

"So, where were we?" she asked.

"I was about to say that I'd have thought you'd insist on using Air Force personnel if we need a consult."

Tricia very nearly lost her appetite thinking about her reasoning. "Actually, I'm in a unique situation with this investigation," she began, putting down her fork. "Travis, I don't know who to trust because we don't know exactly what happened to give Ian away. We don't know if he confided in someone—the wrong someone—and was betrayed. If he questioned the wrong person. Was seen in the wrong place. Ian was a top-notch investigator. I can't see him being careless, so my money's on outright betrayal."

"So, you're willing to use me and my contacts because you figure I couldn't have been involved."

How to explain while making sure he kept his family, or at least most of it, in the dark? "I trust you. I trust

Sam. And I'll trust your judgment, but I don't want to chance a leak on this investigation. If your parents, sister and cousins believe we're together for personal reasons, along with the whole Montgomery extended family, our cover will be solid gold."

"Yes, but my dad is someone I often bounce ideas off of."

She just couldn't tell Travis his father was a suspect whose activities might put his entire family in danger. But neither could she risk him talking to the man who was her prime suspect as Hadley's local connection.

Known for thinking fast on her feet, Tricia countered with "Travis, you can't put your father in that sort of spot. You saw how your mother reacted to seeing us together. If he knows we aren't really seeing each other and doesn't tell her—"

Travis winced. "Good point. The eruption of Vesuvius would look like a seismographic ripple. Okay, Dad stays out. And in the same vein, Sam stays in the dark about us. Though I do owe him for the salad. I was hoping for Mom's lasagna. Sam can know we're working together on this but not that the investigation is all that's going on between us. No sense risking his neck with my mother, too," he said, and grimaced as he watched the esteemed lady flitting around her customers but steering clear of *them*—obvious in her wish to leave them alone together.

"You're so lucky to have a mother like her. Protecting her is a good idea."

"Yeah, Mom's great." He leaned forward and took

her hand. Tricia just managed not to jump out of her skin. His head was bent so she couldn't see his eyes. He turned her hand over and caressed her wrist with his thumb. Lightning shot through her veins and she repressed a gasp with an effort. She stared at the top of his head, then he looked up and grinned. Did he know what his touch was doing to her? She hoped not!

"So, did you get anywhere with Johnston and those logs you wanted a copy of?" he asked quietly.

Feeling like a fool for her reaction, Tricia nodded and swallowed, reminding herself that his touch and interest were for an audience only. Carefully she pulled her hand from his. "Captain Johnston was pretty sure none of the other Buccaneers would be around Meadow Lake Airport today. General Fielding sent him off base to speak at the academy, so he'll have plenty of extra time to get up to the airfield and back. We decided if he asked to see the logs, it would arouse less suspicion than if I got a warrant for them."

"Do you think someone at the airport is in on this whole thing? Could that be where your leak was?" He took her hand again, gently stroking it.

Keeping his voice pitched low to keep the conversation private gave his voice an incredibly sexy timbre. And he was still gazing into her eyes as if daring her to pull away or at least object to his attentions. She was made of stronger stuff than that! Trying to drive her around the bend, was he? Well, she'd show him.

Idly Tricia began tracing the fine veins on the back of his hand with the fingertips of the hand he wasn't holding. "I'm not sure if that's where Ian made his mistake but the general and I were worried about it. Captain Johnston will get word of a sudden family emergency as soon as he gets back to Peterson later today. General Fielding is sending him somewhere safe until all this is over. Even I don't know where he's headed."

"So where do *we* go from here?" he asked.

Travis's ambiguous question blasted away all her self-delusions about her feelings for him. Because all of a sudden she knew she wanted his question to be about them and not the investigation.

Chapter Six

Tricia's eyes widened, arresting his attention. They caught the light from one of the Stagecoach Café's rear windows and shone with the subtle mahogany undertone he'd always found fascinating. "What?" she asked, clearly bewildered by whatever he'd said.

What *had* he said?

Unfortunately, his mind was a blank slate, erased by her touch and those incredible eyes. Her confusion and the sudden increased strain in the air snapped Travis out of what felt like a trance. He dropped her hand, pulling his own from under her torturing fingertips. What had he said to put that look on her face? Had he given away the feelings her touch caused?

"Uh…what do you mean 'what'?" he replied, trying to cover his own scrambled thoughts.

She frowned, her lush eyebrows drawn together in deep contemplation "You asked where we go from here. I…um…wasn't sure what you meant."

He'd been asking about the investigation, hadn't he? Of

course he had. He'd been trying to make her uncomfortable in payment for forcing him into this charade. Then she'd tried to turn the tables on him. And she had. Distracting him, muddling his brain with her touch. But his question hadn't been about them. It couldn't have been.

Because if it was, he was in big trouble.

Travis forced the grin he always used to hide his true feelings. "Why, sweet cakes, surely you knew I meant the investigation. It's all we have in common these days, after all."

Her hands now in her lap, Tricia's gaze slid from his to her lap then she nonchalantly twisted a bit and picked up her purse. "What else would you have meant?" she asked, her head bent as she looked for something in the recesses of her pocketbook. Then she looked back up, her demeanor all business. "Something seemed to be bothering you, that's all. We were talking about Captain Johnston, so I thought you might have had plans to talk to him yourself. I wondered if his leaving had put a crimp in your thought processes."

She was so cool. So unrattled. There was no way he was going to let on that her touch had nearly undone him. "It might have been a good idea for me to have a shot at talking to our whistle-blower, but for his safety I see the merit of shipping him out. He's taken quite a chance already, considering what happened to Kelly."

She nodded. "And he's been keeping logs of the mileage the others put on the F-100. It'll be a help. I thought if I could find out what towers they've been checking in at and where they were when they filed their amended flight plans, I might be able to pinpoint their destination with the approximate mileage figures I'm going to get from Captain Johnston."

"Why not just plant a global positioning tracker in the plane and watch these guys from orbit? You'd know where they land in seconds."

"I thought of that but first I watched Captain Edwards last week before his weekend flight. He had an electronic bug detector of some sort that looked pretty sophisticated. He used it to do a thorough sweep of the plane before taking off. I'm pretty sure he was using it to make sure he hadn't picked up a GPS tail of some sort. Captain Taylor did the same thing this week."

Travis straightened a bit as his heart sped up of its own accord. And he knew why. Much as he once again hated to admit it, he hated the idea of her skulking around after the men who'd executed Kelly. She had to be competent or she'd never have risen to the rank of major, but still…

"So we do this the old-fashioned way," he said before letting his thoughts get away from him. "Did you tail Edwards the way you did Taylor after he landed?"

She nodded. "But it was fully night by the time he left the base. I lost him on Interstate 25."

"When do you meet Johnston to pick up the logs and info from the airport?"

She checked her watch. "1500. At the giraffe exhibit in Cheyenne Mountain Zoo."

"That should give us enough time to get to my place so I can start downloading some maps. Then we'll be all set to use what Johnston has for us." He pointed to her last piece of manicotti. "You going to finish that?"

Tricia tilted her head, her lips curving into a teasing grin. His heart stuttered, thudding in an entirely different way than it had only moments earlier. Why did she still affect him in all these strange but familiar ways?

"Since you finished your veggies," she said at length, "I suppose it's okay if I give you my leftovers."

He scowled at her but wasted no time in snatching up the meager remains of his mother's five-star cooking. He would have thought as thin as Tricia was she'd never be able to pack away as much food as she had while they'd talked. Allison had always eaten like a bird. What kind of a woman didn't worry about her weight? It was a female thing, wasn't it?

"Aren't you worried about your weight?" he wondered aloud.

Tricia blinked. "Are you saying you think I'm fat?" she demanded, offended.

"I didn't say anything about your weight. I was talking about your appetite. You're healthy looking. I wouldn't say fat. I didn't say fat."

"I really have to tell you, Travis, it's a good thing this isn't a real date or you'd be wearing that manicotti instead of chewing it. Healthy is a synonym for plump."

"Quit acting like a woman and reading things into what I say."

Tricia stood. "I'm afraid you've teamed up with a woman and you're stuck with me for the duration. Excuse me while I visit the *women's* room."

Travis scowled. What was with her? He'd only been making conversation. He had *not* called her fat.

All of a sudden his mother stood at his side. "Tricia looked upset. What did you do?" she insisted on knowing.

Just what he needed. A second female on his back! And as far as he knew, not one of her children had ever gotten away with "None of you business" as a reply to Lidia Vance.

"She didn't seem upset to me," he lied.

"Don't you lie to me, Travis Maxwell Vance. Lie to yourself but not to me. What happened?"

He shrugged. "I said she ate a lot. She said I thought she was fat."

His mother tilted his chin up so he had to look at her. "*Stupido!* My son is *stupido!* You go across the road to that flower shop and buy her some flowers. Now."

"Do you know what that florist charges? She's a thief in florist's clothing. It isn't necessary anyway. Tricia wasn't that upset."

"You called the girl fat and—"

"I said she looked healthy!"

"Oh, excuse me, Mr. Casanova! To a woman that means *fat!* Go, or for a month you'll eat salad every time you see me. Understand?"

Knowing he'd never win this argument, Travis groaned, stood and went across the street. Halfway there he decided it was possible—just possible—that he may have been a little grouchy and that maybe he'd taken out his mood on Tricia. He should have just said what he'd thought—that she ate a lot for someone so thin—instead of what he had said. Remembering Allison's dieting frenzy after Natalie was born, he certainly didn't want the guilt of sparking that kind of reaction in someone who didn't have a pound to spare.

In college he used to stop and buy Patty flowers from a flower vendor on campus and he recalled her delight in them. Perhaps Mom was right. Flowers would soothe her annoyance at him and put them back on track to a smooth working relationship. As he stepped inside the shop his gaze fell on a profusion of violets in a refrigerator case. He'd given her a small bouquet of them for the spring dance in college. "How much for some of those violets?" he asked the woman behind the counter.

"Actually, we got them in for a wedding this weekend. I'm not sure I can spare any," she replied cagily.

He sighed. "How much to tie a bunch of them together with a bow?"

She named her outrageous price and he nodded reluctantly. The woman belonged in an orange jumpsuit picking up trash off the sides of the roads! Five minutes later and twenty bucks poorer, he jogged back across the street vowing to deduct the stupid flowers as a business expense.

Tricia's eyes went all smoky when she looked up and caught sight of the flowers. "Here. Don't go losing weight on my account," he growled, and stuck them in her water glass rather than chance touching her as he handed them to her.

Tricia picked up the bunch and bent her head to sniff

them. Then she let out an unladylike snort and grinned crookedly. "You sweet-talker, you. Next, you'll be picking up the tab."

"Well, of course I am. I'll get to deduct both lunch and the flowers from my taxes." He checked his watch. "Maybe we should get a move on. We'll run by my place and download those maps, then we'll get over to the zoo early. That way we can have a good look around first and make sure Johnston isn't being followed when he gets there."

She nodded and gathered up her purse and her violets. "Good thinking…and the zoo will look like the perfect first date to everyone," she added with a slight flourish of the flowers.

He gritted his teeth, snatched up the check and went to pay his tab. *Sam's* tab, he reminded himself, was growing exponentially. And he'd owed Travis big-time already.

Chapter Seven

This was her first visit to Cheyenne Mountain Zoo. When Tricia attended the academy, fear of seeing Travis after running into Allison in a Manitou Springs drugstore one day had kept her pretty much on Air Force property. She'd spent any of her meager time off in Denver or at the family home of a close friend during her years at the academy. That was another reason this assignment was so fraught for her and something she hadn't mentioned to Travis yet.

Elliott Harrison, one of the Buccaneers, was the friend who'd held her together in those days when her world had narrowed to the academy compound. In the dark days after Travis's graduation when he'd suddenly eloped with Allison, Tricia met an Air Force recruiter by chance on campus. The life he'd described as a military investigator and the military world itself sounded as if it was for her. Rules and discipline. Restful and uncomplicated.

She would have no more worries about whether the money from her mother would last until graduation and until she found a full-time job. And she could even give up the part-time job she'd taken to stretch the money further. All she had to do was get in. The requirements were tough but her grades were excellent and her congressman was more than happy to get her the appointment. There'd been that one drawback. The Air Force Academy was in Travis's hometown.

But she'd been sure Allison would remain in school and near her adoring parents in Pennsylvania and that Travis would join the police force in Philadelphia or one of its surrounding communities. She'd never thought Allison's parents would let her give up her education or move to far-away Colorado. What Tricia hadn't counted on was that a baby was on the way or that Travis would take his pregnant wife back to Colorado Springs to live.

Then had come the surprise encounter with Allison. She'd gloated about her happy marriage and the baby on the way. Tricia had understood her error in judgment only then. She was stuck in Colorado Springs, having joined the branch of the service that would practically guarantee her a bird's-eye view on the life that could have been hers. Tricia had also come to understand the cruelest fact of all. She'd set herself up for further heartbreak after the argument with Travis by confiding in her roommate in the first place.

It turned out that Allison had always wanted Travis. She'd seen no reason why she couldn't have him and anything else she wanted. And Tricia had given her the keys to his heart by telling her Travis desperately wanted a wife and family. So desperately that he said he wasn't willing to wait for her. He hadn't had to wait a single day for Allison. She'd been ready, willing and emotionally ready to give Travis what he needed—all the things Tricia was not yet ready to give any man.

After that meeting with Allison Vance, the first person she'd seen when she'd returned to the academy was Elliott Harrison. He'd held her as she'd cried for the life she'd led and the one she'd wanted one day but had had to turn down because that time wasn't now. And a friendship had been formed that had spanned ten years, twelve duty stations between the two of them, a marriage on the rocks and the death of his recalcitrant wife following the birth of his son. And now Tricia was in the middle of an investigation of that friend and his compatriots. She prayed that, evidence to the contrary, Elliott wasn't involved.

She hadn't planned to hide their friendship from anyone, but after the general's reaction to her previous relationship with the Vances and his lack of faith in her judgment, she just wasn't ready for another confrontation with anyone. She'd pick her time and slide it into the conversation with Travis. And continue praying Elliott was innocent.

Pushing troubling thoughts to the back of her mind, and though there was another purpose for being at the zoo, Tricia let the festive atmosphere soothe her. They positioned themselves between the outdoor aviary and the monkey cage, giving them a wonderful view of the giraffe enclosure. That way they could keep an eye out for Captain Johnston and make sure no one had followed him.

It was early yet, so she took a few moments to watch the cavorting monkeys then she looked away to glance down at the pretty little bunch of violets she'd tucked in the top of her purse. Such a sweet gesture delivered in such a brusque way. She smiled. What a perfect illustration of Travis as he was now. It was as if he were uncomfortable with any of the softer emotions, reserving them only for his mother.

Yet when she'd gone in search of the bathroom at his house, she'd tried to open two different closed doors along the hallway and had found them locked. One she was sure must have been the master suite and she assumed the other door, decorated with painted flowers, pink ribbons and ballet slippers, had been Natalie's room. Since there was little purpose in locking an empty room, Tricia also assumed the rooms were probably the way they'd been when Allison and their daughter were killed. That those rooms sat undisturbed while all the other furniture was gone was poignant and made so clear how wounded he still was. It nearly broke her heart.

In short—Travis wasn't as tough as he wanted everyone to think.

"You look awfully down-hearted all of a sudden. No, don't tell me. You feel bad for the zoo animals," Travis said, his eyes scanning the crowd, alert to everything going on around them but also revealing a knowledge of her character that matched her knowledge of his.

She shrugged, unwilling to give away her feelings for him and the sorry state of his life. But now that he'd brought up the monkeys… "It is sort of sad," she told him as the monkey chatter picked up momentarily. "They probably live a better, more certain life here than in the wild. Meals on time. No one hunting them. Free medical care." She chuckled a little, knowing she was stretching the metaphor. "But at what price? They have no freedom. They can't even really choose a mate." She shrugged, ending on a more serious note and seeing a bit of a similarity of the life she'd described to the military one. It was something she promised herself to think about and pray about later.

"Yeah, well, maybe people would be better off that way," Travis mused. "Me? I'll take certainty any day. In this world, you never know when someone is hiding just around the corner ready to smack you upside the head."

"Or when life's about to hand you your dream come true. You're forgetting that part of the equation."

"Right. You find your dream come true and it turns into a nightmare." He snapped his fingers saying, "Just like that." As if to punctuate his words, a bird screeched in the background.

"Well, yes, but if we all stayed in our safe little boxes, we'd miss all the wonderful special blessings we'd never imagine for ourselves. God is good, Travis, but we have to give Him the opportunity to bless us and time to bring things around."

Travis scowled, clearly unconvinced. She noticed a young couple. Each of them had a child by the hand and her heart ached for the family she could have had with Travis had she not had so much baggage left from her dysfunctional childhood and still so much growing up to do when he'd asked her to marry him. If only she'd known the Lord then and could have just laid her life and pain at His feet. She knew what she was talking about. She'd practically lived Travis's life but in reverse.

When Travis had become angry over her stance on marriage, she'd given up on him just as Travis had given up on life. She hadn't contacted him to try working things out. She'd assumed it was up to him to come to her. She'd simply gone away, licked her wounds and abdicated the responsibility of her love for him and let him ruin his life. He deserved it, she'd told herself when she'd learned about him and Allison. They both did. But she'd been wrong.

As the couple moved on toward the giraffe enclosure, Tricia noticed another twosome—a foursome really—who happened to go to Good Shepherd. And they were the perfect illustration of the point she was trying to make with Travis.

"See that woman over there with the little girl and the man next to her who's got his hand on the boy's shoulder. That's Jerry and Eva Cagney. They attend Good Shepherd. They lost a child to a congenital disease that it turned out any children of theirs would have. But they put their fate in the Lord's hands and adopted those two children even though they were afraid to love another child they could lose if the biological parents changed their minds. They took a chance on life—on God—and were rewarded with a beautiful family."

"And the moral of your story is?"

"Exactly what I said. Life is worth taking a chance on." Travis frowned thoughtfully and turned away. "Is that your pilot?" he asked, nodding toward a man walking purposefully toward the giraffe enclosure.

She sighed. Maybe she wasn't meant to help Travis. She'd thought that might be why the Lord had put him in her life again. To give her a chance to make up for practically delivering him into Allison's hands. "Yes, that's Captain Johnston," she said and, after watching the crowd for a short while, started forward.

"Finally. We've wasted enough time here today," he muttered, and followed.

Tricia sighed in frustration and stopped a few feet in front of Captain Kevin Johnston. "How'd it go, Captain?" she asked, returning his salute.

"Fine, ma'am," he said in his down-home Southern accent.

"You two aren't in uniform. Could we can the military protocol?" Travis grumbled. "The idea is to be *in*conspicuous."

"Sorry," Johnston said, his eyes darting about.

"Relax," Travis told him. "You weren't followed. Now what happened?"

"I told the secretary at the airfield that I'm trying to figure out how efficient the engines on the Sabre are. She didn't bat an eye when I asked for copies of everyone's logs."

"But do you think she'll mention this to any of the Bucs?" Tricia asked, worried about the integrity and secrecy of the investigation.

"Let's keep on walking," Travis said, "and try to look like you're having a good time, kiddies."

The captain gave an unconvincing smile and continued as if Travis hadn't spoken. "She didn't seem to think it was an unusual request and besides, she doesn't usually run into any of us. She works a strict ten-hour day, Monday through Thursday. Another woman works Friday through Sunday. Since we all take leave on weekends to fly the plane, I doubt any of them run into her often. Before today, I'd only seen her once nearly a year ago, on the day we signed the lease on the hangar for the jet. And I did what you suggested, ma'am. I left a bunch of fuel calculations on my flights lying around in my quarters as insurance."

Tricia grinned. "That's terrific. We may just get away with this."

The three of them continued to stroll, this time by the aviary. "Do you still think I need to disappear, then?" Captain Johnston asked.

Tricia took a long look at him. General Fielding had already lost one man on this case, and didn't plan on losing another. "We don't intend to risk your life. You'll get a nice paid vacation until this is over."

"That doesn't matter to me, ma'am. I just want to fly. I haven't wanted to be anything but an Air Force pilot from the day I turned ten. I was helping my daddy plow when a military jet cracked the sound barrier overhead. Most of the other Buccaneers like the high life and the glory of being pilots. I guess that's why they're doing whatever it is they're doing. Maybe it's the money. The Sabre—she really cuts into our pay. I guess they just didn't want to sacrifice the life they had for her. Harrison, I'm not sure about. This doesn't fit at all with him."

"Is that the info?" Travis asked, pointing to a back-pack Captain Johnston had slung over his shoulder.

The pilot nodded, dropped his shoulder so it slid down his arm. He looked down at the blue backpack, shook his head and handed it to Tricia. "Get them, ma'am. I was mighty proud of that plane and they've turned her into something ugly. Worse thing with this is I know I'm bound to lose her."

She hadn't even thought of that. She put a comforting hand on his arm. "I'm sorry, Captain. I don't know what will happen but I'm afraid the Feds will impound her. I promise I'll do my level best to get them, though. I hope that helps," she told the captain, trying not to think of Elliott lumped in with the rest. "You know where you're supposed to go from here?" she asked.

"Yes, ma'am. I go to Peterson, take a message from the guard at the gate then go right to see General Fielding. After that he'll tell me where to head and tell General Hadley that there's a problem with my sister. Since I have a sister who disappeared with a biker a few years ago, the other Bucs ought to confirm that it's possible I was called home."

"Good luck, Captain, and thanks again for all your help."

He shook his head. "Just doing my duty, ma'am," he said, sadness in his voice and the stoop of his shoulders as he turned and walked away.

Travis looked after him. "Poor guy. Just goes to prove that no good deed goes unpunished."

"You're a cynic, Travis Vance. You know that?"

"I'm a realist. I call them as I see them. Let's get back to my place and take a long look at this stuff."

Four hours later they had a conglomeration of maps of the United States as well as Mexico, Central America and northern South America all taped together like a giant jigsaw puzzle and tacked to the dining room area wall. Travis was marking each pilot's progression from tower to tower using different colored pins for each flight. Tricia, at the calculator, had begun to subtract the mileage of the known portions of the flights. Until they plotted and accounted for those, they couldn't move to the next step of triangulating the places that could be the final destination. And all of that was complicated all the more because there were return trips to Meadow Lake included within the true mileage Johnston had logged.

Travis's phone rang and he answered it on the third ring. "Vance," he said almost distractedly. His eyes widened a bit. "Oh, hi, Dad."

Tricia stiffened. Would he stick to his promise and keep his father in the dark? This was the most dangerous part of her assignment with Travis. If he broke her confidence and his father was guilty, it could very well get her killed.

"Actually Tricia's here right now. Dinner? I don't know. I wasn't planning anything, no, but it's a little early. No. Not yet. Yeah, I'm sure. Maybe in a while. Okay, see you." He hung up.

"You turned down dinner? We're supposed to be dating, Travis. You came off like you don't want me included in your life."

He sighed, annoyed. "I was pretending to keep you to myself. Almost like I'm embarrassed to be seen with you—and don't go taking that the wrong way. I know what I'm doing where they're concerned. My parents know me. They know I don't date. They know I've been telling them for years I like my life just the way it is. A complete about-face in one day and acting as if they haven't been preaching at me for years would be too much for them to swallow."

The general wanted her to infiltrate his family. Though the idea of spying on the Vances made her uncomfortable, she wouldn't disobey an order, and she would stop short of nothing to hang the person or persons responsible for Ian Kelly's murder.

"Fine. Just don't play reluctant suitor too long or you'll blow our cover."

"You have the next leg of this flight calculated yet?" he asked, ignoring her warning.

Out of patience with the poor lighting and spartan atmosphere, she snapped, "No. I don't. I'm cross-eyed. I'm hungry. I feel as if I'm sitting on a log in a cave. Can't you at least get something more comfortable for company to sit on out here than a folding chair?"

"I don't have company."

She just couldn't stay in that house for one more second. "I can see why. I'm calling it a night." She picked up her purse and nearly fled. At the front door she turned back. "Honestly, Travis, the hair shirt after ten years is a bit much. You really need to move on."

"What do you know about it?"

"I know enough to recognize a pathetic life when I see one. And this…" She gestured to the two rooms that were the center of Travis's world—AdVance Security. "This is pathetic with a capital *P*. Take a hint. When military housing is homier than your own, it's time for a change. Call me and we'll get together tomorrow…at my place. Right now I need some fresh air and somewhere comfortable to sit."

Chapter Eight

Travis stumbled to the kitchen, still half-asleep, having worked late into the night mapping out many of the known flight plans of the pilots. Sunshine poured into the kitchen window as he poured himself a cup from the already-brewed coffee in his timer-controlled pot, his one luxury in life.

He set down his coffee as a stabbing pain in his back caught him unaware. Irritated, he rotated his hips trying to relieve the familiar backache. "That futon's gotta go," he growled to Cody who'd jumped to his feet at Travis's sharp hiss of pain.

And then he stopped and thought—really thought this time—about Tricia and her parting remarks. He looked around at what had once been a pretty cool-looking house. A house he and Allison had entertained in frequently. With new eyes he saw what his grief, guilt and anger had done to his life.

Sinking to a bar stool, Travis scrubbed his face with his hand and grimaced. At first he'd gotten rid of the furniture because it was too much of a day-in-and-day out, in-your-face reminder of people and good times gone forever. He'd had intentions of replacing it, but that had never happened. Instead he'd retreated into the back corner of the house and had stayed there. As AdVance had grown it had taken over his world and his home, filling the void he'd allowed his loss and guilt to create.

Now, years later, with the exception of his business contacts and occasional visits with his family, he'd become a hermit. One of those ridiculously sad Western legends who used to hide from life up in hills—just like him.

"Point made, sweet cakes. My house is pathetic. My life is pathetic. *I'm* pathetic."

Head down, Travis walked to the door of the master suite, reached above the frame and pulled down the key. Unlocking it, he closed his eyes, took a deep breath and walked in for the first time in nearly ten years. When he opened them again and looked around at the perfectly preserved past, he didn't feel the sharp pang he'd expected. Though the anger at Allison was still there somewhere, somehow both anger and the guilt over her death had become a dull burning that was more shadow than the substance of pain.

Perfectly preserved, the room lay before him. He routinely unlocked the doors to both bedrooms for the cleaning woman who came in once a month so it was relatively dust-free. But the curtains at the windows were faded and the room smelled stale. Just like his life. Sam was right. He might as well have been buried with them. They all thought he grieved for Allison. But guilt and anger were not grief. He felt responsible for both deaths but it was Natalie, caught between the parents she'd adored, who owned all his grief. She'd been a pawn in Allison's campaign to have life follow the road *she* chose no matter whose dreams she bulldozed under in the process.

He should move on. Sleep in this bed. Move his clothes into this closet and dresser. Shower in this bath. He knew he should. But he turned away, walked back out and closed the door. Maybe another day. Just not today. Travis looked down at the key in his hand and replaced it on the molding without locking the door. Today that felt like enough.

He touched the tiny ring at the base of his throat, then he went to call Tricia. Yeah, today it was enough. And though he didn't know why, annoying as she was, calling Tricia felt right, too.

"Major Streeter," she said, her voice slightly hushed, but clean and precise. And irritating. Where was all the soft-spoken girl he'd loved listening to? Where was the smile that had always been in her voice like a whisper on a warm breeze? Where was the reserve that had made her seem subdued and even a bit timid? He'd never have poked fun at *her*—never had. He'd just wanted to protect that girl. But this woman she'd become made him want to spar with her and stick pins in her self-assurance.

"Your idea stinks," he said without preamble. "I was up all night. We need more from each of the control towers they were in contact with or were supposed to be. Eventually, with that information added to the mix, we may find out what country they're coming out of but not exactly where they land. We can get your pilots easy enough with what we know if we stake them out and document their movements, but we'll never get to the other end of the pipeline this way or to the general—if he's the one controlling this."

"I hoped…" She sighed. "Then I guess we'd better come up with something better although I still have to do the mapping for trial. Even circumstantial evidence that won't convict them by itself can help sway a jury in the right direction and stiffen sentences."

"We'll get back to it another time, then. Which one of the Buccaneers is slated to fly out this weekend?"

"Captain Elliott Harrison. I'm praying he's not one of them. We went through the academy together. He was such a nice guy. I can't see him running drugs or having a hand in Ian Kelly's murder."

He could hear pain in Tricia's voice. Travis once again found himself unaccountably fighting unreasonable jealousy. He paced back down the hall and stared at the maps that should have been impressed in his brain by then. It may as well have been a blank wall. She had his emotions bouncing all over the place and he just couldn't keep up. Even her mention of prayer aggravated him. Which aggravated him all the more because he was usually able to ignore references to God from his family—and that happened practically every time he saw them! He even managed to ignore God himself.

"So you don't have solid evidence on all of them."

His tone added an unspoken, sarcastic "big deal." "Does that mean you don't think this guy's guilty?"

At the other end of the line Tricia sighed again. "That's the thing about circumstantial evidence. It can be wrong. It can be right. If I nail these guys, Elliott Harrison among them, I want to be on solid ground. I'll know for sure by tonight if Elliott's involved."

"You intend to stake out and watch the plane later today?"

"Well…if he uses the equipment Captains Taylor and Edwards used, then he must be in on it. If not—"

"If not," Travis chimed in, "it looks as if we have the weekend off. He's one of the pilots whose past flights I didn't get a chance to start mapping yet." Travis turned from the map and walked to his front window, which afforded him a majestic view of Pikes Peak. But today it failed to calm his restless spirit. There was a time he'd have said the Lord was trying to warn him that something was wrong—but he no longer listened for that sort of message. He and God weren't on "speaking" terms these days.

"I hope for Elliott's sake he's not involved," Tricia said. The phone crackled at the other end as if she, too, were moving restlessly. "It's possible he's just not paying close attention the way Captain Johnston was to the mileage other pilots are putting on the plane. He has a lot on his mind these days."

Travis wanted to say he hoped so, too—for her sake. But the words stuck in his throat, as did the knowledge of her friendships with so many men. What was wrong with him? He hadn't for one second ever felt jealous of Allison. And he didn't think he'd been this way about Tricia back in college. What did that say about him? That he'd regressed maybe, he thought, disgusted with himself all over again.

"Does Harrison have a family? Do any of them?"

"Walters is married to a real wild child. She doesn't fit in with any of the officers' wives, which could be a hint to his personality. Elliott Harrison was recently widowed. He has an infant son who lives in Phoenix with his mother and father. I'm telling you, Travis, this doesn't fit with Elliott. In fact, I talked to him last night at the O Club. He's trying to sell his share of the jet and is just hanging in with the Air Force until this tour is up. The rest of them are bachelor jet jocks. Fly high, straight and on the edge—and play even closer to the edge."

He grinned at the distaste in her voice. He imagined she'd had more than one run-in with the macho-pilot type in her military career. "And you can't wait to knock them off," he mused, thinking about her take on the men under investigation.

"They give the Air Force a bad name. Military bases try to add positive influences to the communities they're near, not destroy them," she said, her voice distracted and filled with something he couldn't interpret.

Travis understood her feelings about the pilots. He and Sam felt the same way about dirty cops but that didn't explain the faraway tone in her voice. "Where are you and what's wrong?"

"I'm in a vacant slot next to the chaplain's office. It's

on the edge of officers' housing. Harrison still lives there even though he's alone now. I've been watching his place since 0530. And I'm worried. He was on duty as of 0700 and he didn't leave. Something's…*wrong,*" she said.

Travis felt a shiver run down his spine and that feeling of impending doom flared again. "I thought we were supposed to be in this together."

"We are."

"First, if we're in this together, then why are you there alone? Kelly was killed on that base by at least one of the people you're investigating. I'm on my way. Get me on the base."

"Travis, I can't leave where I am to meet you at the gate. I'm telling you, something's wrong here."

Travis's heartbeat picked up, thundering in his ears. This wasn't good. He didn't like feeling vulnerable because he was afraid for Tricia. But there seemed nothing he could do to make the feeling go away short of finding a way to protect her. "Okay, *I'll* find *you,*" he told her.

"The chaplain's office is number nineteen."

"Okay. Stay there and we'll check Harrison's place together."

"I may have to follow him if he comes out."

"No!"

"Travis, this is my job. I'll be careful. And maybe you shouldn't try to get on base. You'll just call attention to yourself."

"I'll be there in fifteen or twenty minutes, and don't

you tell me what to do if you won't listen to reason," Travis said, and hung up.

He'd taken the precaution of getting General Fielding's number from Tricia and now he was glad he had. He hit the call button on his cell phone as he grabbed his weapon out of the closet to strap it on. He had Fielding on the phone by the time he was headed out to his drive.

"Travis Vance here," he said by way of introducing himself once the general's secretary connected him with Fielding.

"So my secretary tells me. What can I do for you, Mr. Vance?"

"I need to get on base," he explained as he opened the door to his Firebird.

"And why is that?"

"Because you assigned Patricia Streeter to take on six trained soldiers by herself. She's alone right now staking out and watching the home one of these guys on the base where Major Kelly was killed. And I've got a *bad* feeling about it."

"I suppose I could leave word at the gate, but I need to casually mention an excuse to allay any speculation. I can't have you coming to see me. It could jeopardize this ruse you two are using to be seen together."

"Then say I need to talk to the chaplain about my relationship with Tricia."

"Exactly what is your relationship with Major Streeter?"

Travis felt his blood boil. "The one you shoved down

my throat, pal. I didn't like it. I *don't* like it. Nor do I want it, but I'm in now, and you can't pull back by withholding help. Either set me up with the guard at the gate or you're about to have a breach in security. And I'll make it so blatant, the president's going to be asking for your head! And I'm armed. Got it?"

General Fielding chuckled. "She was right. You're nothing like your brother. I'll see that the guard at the gate waves you through. What are you driving?"

"A dark green '69 Firebird."

"Consider it done. And tell Major Streeter I want to meet you."

Travis hung up without acknowledging the order. Fielding wasn't *his* general and he had no intention of kowtowing to the man the way Tricia seemed to. All he wanted as he sped toward Peterson AFB was to nail this drug ring, syndicate, cartel or whatever it was that was flooding Colorado Springs's streets with poison. Then he'd get back to his life.

Except that wasn't likely to happen, he reluctantly admitted as he gunned the engine, easily controlling the car as it climbed the ramp onto the interstate. Hadn't he already acknowledged earlier that his life before Tricia stormed back into it had become pretty barren and hollow? He really might as well have died with Allison and Natalie for all the living he'd been doing.

But he felt alive now. He just wasn't sure he was happy about it. What he was was furious that the option had been taken out of his hands. He'd been content—if numb—but now, like blood beginning to flow into a limb too long asleep, he was painfully aware of life teeming all about him. Of all he'd missed.

Of all he'd lost.

His mind whirling with haunting images and dark thoughts, Travis soon came to the big wooden sign at the front gate of the base. He forced his mind to the problem at hand.

Major Patricia Streeter.

His new "girlfriend."

His old love.

As the general promised, the SP at the gate waved Travis right on through. He stopped a young fresh-faced airman and asked directions to the chaplain's office and parked outside. And for the second time in less than a week he found himself nearly knocked off his feet by the woman occupying way too much of his thoughts of late.

"Where's the fire?" he demanded, his hands instinctively gripping Tricia's slim shoulders.

"I told you. Something's wrong at Elliott's. I'm going over there."

"No. *We're* going over there. You're going to introduce me to your friend because I'm jealous of the time you spent talking to him at the O Club last night."

Tricia tilted her head up, her eyes widening. Then she nodded nearly imperceptibly. "Right. A cover story. Thanks for thinking it out. Let's go." She stepped away from him then reached up and took his descending hand.

He frowned when his heart took off and his blood pressure shot up the scale. Was she going to start that again?

As if she'd read his mind, Tricia smirked. "Got to keep up appearances. Right?"

Not trusting himself to answer, he gave her a sharp nod and turned around leading the way back out the front door of the building and to his car. Less than two minutes later they climbed back out when Travis parked in front of Harrison's small, well-kept apartment building.

Tricia frowned when she knocked on the front door and no answer came.

"You're sure he was still in there when you came out into the hall to meet me?"

She nodded. "I suppose he could have left while we were on the way here."

"Does this place have a back door?"

She started around the side of the building. "This looks to be laid out like my place. There are back stairs from the upper apartments and a common vestibule with the lower ones."

They entered the vestibule and moved toward the door to the lower unit. Travis tried the door. It swung inward easily. Too easily. Eerily.

He heard Tricia gasp before it registered that Captain Elliott Harrison was on the floor next to the kitchen table. There was a rubber tourniquet wrapped around his arm and a needle on the floor next to him. It looked as if Harrison had taken the easy way out of responsibility for his child and his mistakes.

Chapter Nine

Tricia saw Elliott's leg encased in a flight suit sprawled out on the floor. She pushed past Travis who cursed as he stepped into the room.

"No! Please, Lord, don't let him be dead. He just can't be," she said, dropping next to the pilot who'd been her bulwark during her first months at the academy. She checked for a heartbeat and breathed a slight sigh of relief. There was a weak and thready pulse and he was still taking shallow breaths. "Call 911," she ordered, her voice cracking with strain. "He's alive but just barely."

Travis went immediately to the phone and made the call as Tricia held her friend's hand urging him to fight for the life he'd planned with his son.

"I don't think he's too interested in living, Trish," Travis said quietly from behind her.

Tricia was momentarily surprised at the gentleness in Travis's tone but she knew she'd fall apart if she leaned on him or anyone. "Of course he is. His son is everything to him. He's leaving the military so he can raise him by himself."

"There's a note here on the table that says otherwise," Travis countered, his voice still devastatingly kind.

She felt her strength begin to ebb. "That can't be. I talked to him just last night. He seemed upbeat and sure of his decision. He had so many plans for Teddy and himself. How could I not have seen how desperate he was? I'd really begun to believe he wasn't involved. This just makes no sense."

Travis squatted down next to Elliott. "A positive attitude is sometimes a sign that someone's made the decision to end it all. And who's Teddy?"

"His son," she answered absently, turning her attention back to Elliott Harrison. "Come on, Elliott, hang on for baby Teddy. He needs his daddy. You said it yourself—your parents are too old to raise another wild and woolly Harrison."

"Teddy's a nickname for Edward?" Travis asked inanely as he stared down at the crumpled paper he'd picked up with a handkerchief covering his fingertips.

His question dragged Tricia's attention away from her friend once again and she frowned, then looked back at Elliott. "How'd you know the baby's real name? Teddy is the only way he refers his son."

Travis frowned and turned the note so she could read it. Once again, she dragged her gaze from Elliott's pale face. The penmanship was his but it didn't have its usual beautiful and precise flow of thoughts. It just felt wrong.

"He wrote it but I don't think it was his idea. It

doesn't flow naturally and it looks as if his hand wasn't too steady when he was writing it. 'Tell Edward he's better off with my parents and I miss Debra too much to go on. Her death was too much of a shock to withstand'?" she read aloud in a questioning tone. "Oh, no, no, no."

"It's not true, is it?" Travis asked.

"He and Deb were barely speaking by the time Teddy was born. There was an ugly custody battle brewing. Her death was a shock but he was far from despondent. Relieved is probably closer to the truth, though Elliott would never say so."

"You didn't say anything about that earlier."

"Why speak ill of the dead? She wasn't cut out for military life but not because she hated moving or worried about the danger. She couldn't stand being alone and she found plenty of companionship outside their marriage. He even considered having DNA testing done on the baby, but he changed his mind after she died."

"And no one on base knew all this?"

She shook her head. "It was common knowledge but no one at Cascade tossed it in Elliott's face. She died right after they moved here. Around nearly everyone—especially the Buccaneers—he acted as if he didn't know about the affairs. Pride, I guess. But he talked to me about it."

Elliott's breathing rattled and Travis dropped the rest of the way to his knees. "I think his heart's arresting. Do you know CPR?" he asked as he unzipped Elliott's flight suit.

Tricia simply nodded and scooted to Elliott's head. Just as she reached out to adjust her friend's head, Travis said, "Great. I'll do chest compressions while you help him breathe."

The sound of an ambulance siren pealed in the distance then and she thanked God. As she blew breaths into Elliott's lungs, she prayed for her friend's life to be spared. Moments later a number of paramedics from the Colorado Springs Fire Department rushed in and took over. It wasn't long before they had him stabilized enough to allow him to be transported to Memorial Hospital.

"I'll call Sam. Maybe he can find a way to put a guard on his room." Travis's gaze hardened. "I'm thinking they used heroin. That's what they used on Valenti." Seeing Trish's shaken reaction to his musings, he added, "Harrison still has a chance, Trish."

Tricia nodded and dropped to the sofa, her legs too weak to hold her upright. "If we ask for protection it might tip off the Bucs that we know he didn't do this to himself. I think we need to keep that pretense up to save the case. Let me call General Fielding. He can pretend Elliott's under arrest for the suicide attempt and possession of the drugs."

Travis grimaced. "Would they do that?"

She shrugged. He clearly had no idea how contrary some commanding officers or the military in general could be. "It's happened. Technically the note says Elliott tried to destroy government property—namely himself. General Fielding isn't normally that hard-nosed but he can be a rough taskmaster. It should be a good smoke screen. I'll make the call," she said, reaching for her cell phone.

Tricia felt Travis's gaze on her the whole time she talked to General Fielding and again as she made the difficult call to Elliott's parents. After assuring the elderly Harrisons that everything was being done and that the Air Force would arrange passage for them to Colorado Springs, Tricia dropped her head onto the back of the sofa. With security police from the base on the way to the hospital and that difficult phone call behind her, Tricia was able to loosen her hold on her emotions. She let her eyes drift closed, fighting tears.

"So now we have a murder attempt—one that may or may not be successful—to add to Major Kelly's murder. And we don't know the motive for this one. So where do you want to go from here?" Travis asked.

Tricia was still too shaken by the events of the past few minutes to rally her thoughts, and she didn't like the irritation in his tone. She just stared at him. He was so cool and collected, too. His quick thinking may well have saved Elliott Harrison's life, yet his calm was as maddening as his annoyance. Didn't anything touch him? She knew she was being unprofessional but Elliott was her friend. And he still might die.

"I'm going to the hospital," she snapped. "You poke around wherever you want. Right now I just want to know he's going to live. There's a set of parents in Phoenix who're going to be devastated if he doesn't pull through this. And I'm sorry if Elliott complicated the case but I'm pretty sure he'd rather not be fighting for his life right now, either!"

Travis's lips thinned. "You think I don't know that? That I don't care the guy might die?" He stood and dragged a hand through his hair as he walked away. Then he whirled to face her, anger in his bright green gaze. "I care plenty. But I also know it could have just as easily been you they carried out of here."

Well, that pretty much took the wind out of her sails. And how could she have forgotten that strangely gentle tone he'd taken with her when they'd first found Elliott?

"These guys aren't kidding around," Travis went on, not realizing he was preaching to the choir. "They're deadly serious about keeping their identities safe and, from where I'm sitting, you're the next one in line as a threat," he snapped, pointing at her. "If you hadn't been a friend of Harrison's your cover would have been blown by just having shown up here to save him." He sighed. "At least that's one thing." His gaze sharpened—all business once again. "Or I hope it is. They *do* know you two go way back, don't they?"

"We didn't keep it a secret. And a lot of people saw us at the O Club last night. In fact, we left at the same time." A terrible thought occurred to her. "You don't think they know I'm investigating them, do you? Is this my fault? Did they think he turned on them or came to me about them the way Captain Johnston did?"

"I guess that's where we start. After you check on Harrison, you and I are going to the O Club to stage a little scene."

* * *

They headed back to the base as planned after Elliott Harrison was moved to ICU. The pilot was still in a touch-and-go battle for his life but they couldn't put off the scene at the O Club. Two members of the Air Force's security police stood nearby. Heroin was the drug that had been injected into him, just as Travis had thought. The doctors had no idea if it had been self-inflicted or not but he had a bump on his head that might have happened when he passed out or been inflicted to subdue him. They weren't sure.

Not satisfied with that lukewarm finding, Travis's brother, Sam, quietly called in his own forensic pathologist. The examiner pointed out that the knock on the head was in an unlikely spot for the floor to have caused it and there were bruises on Elliott's arms and shoulders, indicating that he'd been held down by at least two other men. Elliott Harrison had not gone quietly into the oblivion of the coma in which he now lay.

She and Travis cruised back to Peterson in utter silence. When they were nearly there, she realized that since he'd snapped at her in Elliott's living room, they'd spoken only when absolutely necessary. As he pulled the car, achingly familiar from their past together, in front of the O Club at 1530 he asked, "How can you be sure they're going to be here? Three-thirty in the afternoon is a little early to start drinking, isn't it?"

"They'll be here. It's a pattern with most of them. Never less than three of them at a time, actually. Captains Johnston and Harrison were occasionally with them. Enough times that I couldn't clear Elliott. That's why I came here last night. I was hoping to feel him out about what he'd been up to with the plane. Kevin Johnston was in the clear because he'd come to us so—"

"So we go in and take a booth," Travis cut in, clearly not yet in the mood for small talk even about the case. "And I'll get us both a drink." Tricia narrowed her eyes and shook her head interrupting him. "What?" he demanded.

"I don't drink, Travis. That's one thing about me that hasn't changed."

He rolled his eyes. "How virtuous of you. Actually, neither do I. But today you do. We both do. Feed it to the rubber plants, pour it in your purse, I don't care what you do. We need an excuse to go in there so I'm getting you a drink to settle your nerves. Ready?"

"As I'll ever be," she sighed. "Captain Taylor's car's here. So is Reggie Edwards's. And Captains Rule and Walters just pulled in up ahead in that black SUV with the tinted windows."

"So all but one of our boys is here. Perfect," Travis said, and jumped out. Tricia almost blew it right there by opening her own door.

He met her halfway around the back of his car, shaking his head in disgust. "Try to act like this is a date, Major Streeter, and I promise to slam a door in your face when we're alone so you can feel like a good stalwart feminist again."

She blushed, grateful for the dimness. It wasn't feminism but a total lack of dating that was her problem. As they walked away from his car and toward the building, Travis settled his hand on her shoulder, ratcheting up her nerves and her awareness of him with one calculated gesture. Never mind that it was done for a different effect, she still wanted to tell him to keep his hands to himself. She knew, though, for the sake of the entire charade and the investigation that hinged on it that she couldn't. They had to look the part of a new and devoted couple feeling their way through an uncertain and difficult time. Besides, she refused to give him the satisfaction of knowing his touch disturbed her.

They entered the O Club and Travis pointed to a lone booth in a dark corner. He kissed her on the back of the neck, sending a shiver down her spine and a signal to every man in the bar. It was as if he'd branded her as his. And she heartily wished she didn't want it to be true, but she feared she did. Heart pounding, Tricia walked back and slid onto the banquette as Travis suggested. She watched his tense back and shoulders as he wove his way to the bar and prayed her pulse would slow.

Travis headed toward the section of the bar near where the four Buccaneers stood talking. He sized up the pilots who were arranged in varying macho postures along the bar. Pilots were a breed apart, that was for sure. He'd seen each of their photos and had studied their stats so he was easily able to put a name with each of them.

Captain Bruce Taylor, he'd seen in person before the day he and Tricia made contact again. Tall for a pilot and very blond, he looked like an innocent but Travis knew he was anything but, having seen him pass on a bag full of misery that day in the alley.

Captain Reggie Edwards was small, dark and thought the world owed him a free pass. Born to a wealthy influential family, the Air Force was just a stepping stone toward greater things in the political arena. If Travis had his way, Leavenworth would be his next duty station and he'd stay there for the next twenty-five years or so.

Captains Thomas Rule and William Walters were like bookends. Both had brown hair and eyes and were of a medium build and height. The only thing that set them apart from the average pilot was that in each of their personnel files was a notation about a harassment incident involving a female pilot, which stopped each from attaining special top-gun status. Travis wondered if one of them had taken an ordinary gun and ended the life of Ian Kelly, the investigator in the harassment cases.

Travis stepped up to the bar behind Taylor. "Give me a couple Irish whiskeys on the rocks. In fact, make one a double," he told the bartender on a tired sigh.

"Had a bad day?" Rule asked.

"You can't imagine," Travis answered under his breath but loud enough that Taylor could zero in on the sentiment.

Taylor turned around and hooked his elbows on the bar, crossing his feet. "You here with Major Streeter? I don't think I've ever seen her with a guy who wasn't just a pal."

Travis spat out a curse. "Where were you before I made an idiot of myself last night? Tricia and I go back to college but the Air Force got in the way." He reached up and rubbed his neck as if to relieve some tension after a long day. He blew out a disgusted breath. "So when she was late meeting me last night because she'd run into an old friend from the academy, I hit the roof. She claimed he was really depressed about the death of his wife but I wanted proof. So this morning she took me to his place here on base."

The Bucs exchanged significant glances before Walters said, "She was in here last night with one of our buddies. I'd heard she and some guy found him nearly dead this morning. I wondered why anyone would have been at his place when he was supposed to be on duty."

Travis pretended a perplexed frown. "Was he? Tricia was just so mad at me that she was bound and determined to track him down and prove I was acting like a nitwit. That was the first place we went. So we walked in and found him all but dead on the floor. She's really shaken," he said as he picked up the glasses. "And mad as all get-out at some general named Fielding. The hardnose has Harrison under arrest at the hospital and the poor sap's still in a coma. A real compassionate guy, your general."

Again significant glances circulated amongst the pilots. "Under arrest?" Walters asked. "What for?"

"Apparently for trying to destroy government property. Himself, I guess. And for possession. Give the guy a break. He lost his wife and now has a kid to raise so he has to give up his career. And Trish tells me someone told Harrison it may not even be his kid. The guy's taken one hit after another." Travis grinned ruefully. "Well, maybe this will convince her the Air Force isn't more important than giving us a chance. Right?"

Taylor's face relaxed from a frown. "Yeah. Right. Good luck convincing her. I hear she's all career. And tell her thanks for trying to help Harrison. It's not her fault he did what he did. We all feel responsible," the pilot finished by saying as he turned away.

Travis gripped the glasses and walked to the table in the back corner. He could feel his knotted muscles loosen as he got farther away from his quarry. He slid into the booth and set the drinks down. "Pick it up and take a sip if they're watching," he told her, then carefully glanced back at the bar. The quartet of pilots weren't even there anymore but Travis and Tricia didn't dare follow.

Not for the first time Travis wished she wasn't working this case alone. If there were another investigator in position outside, he could have followed them and reported back.

Travis looked back at Tricia and their gazes locked. The next thing he knew everything seemed to empty out of his head. All he could think about was the memory of the soft skin of her nape under his lips when he'd sent her to the booth. And so he found himself wishing for something else. He also wished the next two days didn't look as if they were shaping up as more of the same kind of playacting.

Because it was already getting hard to separate truth from fiction. "So, it looks like we have the weekend off."

Chapter Ten

Tricia's head pivoted toward him. "Off?" she asked as if he'd lost his marbles. "Travis, people don't take a weekend off if they've just begun a relationship. You have to be seen with me. It's our *cover*." She said the last word so carefully emphasizing each syllable that it screamed her opinion of him. And she clearly thought he was a complete idiot who didn't have clue one about how to conduct an undercover investigation.

He'd forgotten was all. He'd looked into her eyes and panicked. Not that he'd tell her that.

"You should invite me to Sunday dinner," she went on, "at your parents' house. Your mother *does* still do Sunday dinner for the family, doesn't she?"

Take her for Sunday dinner? No. Even *he* didn't go to Sunday dinner anymore. "Look, the less we involve my family in this charade the better. You saw my mother's reaction to you yesterday. She'll be asking about our china pattern next."

She turned in her seat to face him. "Are you or are you

not in this thing till the end? I'm not fighting with you every step of the way. You and your stubborn insistence on investigating the Colorado Springs drug problem is what created the need for us to work together. We can always go back to the way it was and risk tripping each other up. But I wish you'd make up your mind."

Fine. When she put it that way. He didn't want her working alone. She probably go and get herself killed the way Kelly had. Then he'd be saddled with a load of guilt because it'd be his fault.

But that didn't mean he had to like it. No, sir. He just wished having her near didn't feel so…so…right.

Wait a minute. What was he saying? Oh, man. He needed some breathing room. And remembering the way she'd jumped all over him when she thought he'd called her fat gave him a great idea. He knew just how to get some space! But he'd try one other thing first. "I didn't say I don't want to work with you," he hedged. "But I can't invite you. It's an after-church thing and I don't go to Good Shepherd anymore."

"As if I don't know that." She shot him a smug look. "Anyone dating me would go to church so I guess you'll be going again for the duration of the investigation."

Okay, now she'd gone too far. He leaned in close and spoke even though his jaw felt as if it had turned to concrete. "Yeah? Well, let me tell you something, Major Streeter. If we're getting into realism, then fix yourself up. I'd never date anyone who looks like you. I mean, look at you. Your hair looks like a military barber cut it with a bowl on your head. And your wardrobe looks like something out of the 'don't' section of a fashion magazine. Do you have to dress like either a dowdy old maid or one of the guys? What do you do? Shop exclusively out of military catalogs? And is wearing a little makeup a crime I haven't heard about? I mean, even an old barn looks better with a new coat of paint."

Her eyes bulged. Her lips thinned. Uh-oh. It looked as if he might get his temporary reprieve. The only trouble was, he'd probably gone way too far. He checked to see if steam was coming from her ears—she was that mad. He'd once heard a well-known comedian describe his wife having a conniption.

It wasn't so funny after all.

"Look…uh…maybe I said too much. I'm sor—"

"Don't," she growled. "Don't you say one more word. Let me tell you something, Travis Maxwell Vance. I live in a man's world. This is a military base, not a cotillion. Why is it okay for men to have serviceable haircuts and wear functional clothes and not have to slather on makeup but women get ridiculed if they do the same thing? And here's something else you probably don't get. If I had painted myself up and dressed out of the 'do' pages of fashion magazines, every man on this base would accuse me of getting these oak leaves by giving away my…my favors…and not from good old-fashioned hard work. Now, you want me 'fixed up.' I want you at church Sunday morning and I want dinner at your parents. So we're going to have a little compromise. Services start at 1100. Meet me at quarter till at the front walk to the church. And hold on to your hat, Travis Vance. Because I'll be looking *fine!*"

Travis watched her slide out of the booth and walk slowly out the door of the O Club. And all he could think was, double uh-oh. He'd really done it now.

It took Tricia fifteen minutes to walk across the base to her car. And with every step she took she vowed Travis Vance would eat his words. Bowl on her head! Her haircut was wash and wear and…and…serviceable!

And you do go to the base barber, a small voice reminded her. *He was right about that.*

So what! Ray Boyle was good at his job. And her clothes, when she wasn't in uniform, were timeless. Classics. They never really went out of style.

That's because they were never really in fashion, either. And you don't have a single civilian outfit suitable for an evening out or even for a dressy day occasion. Church, for instance.

"Fine," she muttered aloud to the fashion critic in her head. She knew just what she was going to do, she decided as she slammed into her apartment and grabbed up the advertisement she'd seen in the weekend section of the paper. "Here you go," she said, and bit her lip before reading aloud the particulars she'd ignored before. "'Spend your Saturday with us. Let Dillard's show you a you you never knew. Free makeover advice from hair to makeup to what to wear on that special date—and all those sure to follow. Saturday from 10:00 a.m. to 5:00 p.m.'" She looked up and caught sight of herself in the mirror. Fingering her straight hair, she shook her head and sighed. Okay. It wasn't a pretty sight. Maybe it was time for a change. She was a major. She'd proven herself. Didn't she outrank ninety percent of the men on the base?

"Dillard's might have their work cut out for them, but Vance, you're about to eat your words!"

Tricia drove to Good Shepherd Church Sunday morning with a new look and her bank balance considerably reduced. Nothing had ever felt so good. And the news from Vance Memorial on Elliott Harrison was pretty good, too. He was conscious, though he had no memory of the events that led to his overdose thanks to a pretty severe concussion. As yet the doctor wouldn't allow him to be questioned but he was still safely under guard.

The day was one of those perfect fall days that only Colorado had to offer. Crisp. Air as clear and clean as a mountain stream, the sun brightening everything, including her mood—a mood that was already pretty sunny.

She arrived at church about twenty minutes before the service as planned. After parking, she positioned herself at the foot of the path to the front door, greeting several church members and enjoying their stunned expressions.

While not entirely comfortable with the stranger who'd stared back at her when the stylist and makeup artist were done, she'd followed their instructions this morning exactly. Tricia had to admit she was rather gratified to look like the kind of person men and women noticed and admired. It was a new and different experience for the foster child who'd learned that if she could stay in the background—unnoticed—she just might get to stay in one place for a while. The only thing she'd ever felt comfortable standing out in was scholastic achievement and her career path but this was something she just might learn to enjoy.

Tricia saw Travis's Firebird wheel around the corner then glide into a spot a bit down the street. He got out, looking handsome and casually elegant in a leather jacket and new jeans as he pocketed his keys and locked the door. She was surprised when he stopped short and turned back to unlock the door, thinking he'd changed his mind. But instead, he reached in and pulled out a dark volume she assumed was a Bible.

"Maybe, Lord, this was an inspired idea," she whispered as he locked the door again and started back down the sidewalk toward her. He walked with a masculine swagger that reminded her of the snow leopards they'd seen at the zoo a few days earlier. Remembering the things he'd said at the O Club Friday, she decided his tongue was as sharp as the leopards' teeth were.

His eyes slid right on by her as he cast his gaze impatiently around. It was clear he didn't know her at first and easy to tell exactly when he realized just who she was. Because he stopped in his tracks and stared, his mouth slightly agape. It was at once gratifying and a little frightening. For a split second, she thought she saw desire flare in his gaze, but then he gave his head an infinitesimal shake and the expression, if it was ever there at all, disappeared.

And the terminal grump was back.

Tricia smoothed her short suede skirt, shifted her

shoulders inside its short matching fawn-colored jacket and moved toward him with a new spring in her step. Her checkbook might show a lower balance but her self-esteem was suddenly high as a kite. And not even grouchy Travis Vance was going to wreck her mood.

When they met, Tricia threw caution to the wind and walked into his arms in a way that forced him to embrace her. She tried not to like the feeling of being so close to him as she kissed him on the cheek. Then, before she got too comfortable, she forced herself to step back but found herself unable to completely break contact. To cover her moment of weakness she used her thumb to wipe off the smudge of a lip imprint her kiss had left behind.

"There, that's better," she said, earning her a growl of annoyance.

"What did you do to yourself?" he demanded next.

Exactly what you said to do, you oaf. She could have said exactly that—even wanted to—but she refused to give him the satisfaction. She would take the knowledge of her trip to Dillard's to her grave. So instead she pinched his cheek—maybe just a little harder than necessary—and laughed. "Why nothing, *darling.*"

"Yeah. Right. You cut your hair even shorter. And you're wearing makeup."

"Oh, that. I was a little overdue for a trim. I've been so busy I just haven't had time for myself." Which was all true. Sort of. She had been busy but for fourteen years, ever since she entered the academy and spent the subsequent years concentrating on her career. And she had needed a trim. She'd just gone to a new hairdresser and he'd suggested highlights and a new spiky, easy-care style along with some makeup suggestions and clothing tips she'd decided to take. That was all that had happened.

"Sam said you wear your uniform to church," he said, his gaze traveling from her pedicure to the highlights in her razor-cut hair.

Uh-oh, she thought. *Busted.* But just as quickly she collected herself and grinned at him, noting that the high heels she now wore took her to nearly eye level with him. It gave her the little extra boost of confidence she needed.

"Why, Travis, I hadn't realized you were so curious about me that you'd have a conversation about my wardrobe with your brother."

He pasted on a gritted-teeth smile. "You're trouble, Major Streeter. A great big bundle of trouble." His eyes flicked over her shoulder. "Oh, great. I see my parents coming our way. Now I guess we have no choice but to get this show on the road."

She glanced over her shoulder. He was right. It was show time. She prayed some personal and spiritual good for Travis would come out of this messed-up charade. Maybe by dragging him to church she'd help him find his way back to his roots. Then he'd feel the comfort of the Lord and get his spiritual life and his life here on earth back on track. Because there had to be some trade-off to hurting Lidia Vance as much as the eventual end of their relationship would.

Tricia held out her hand to Travis. When he took it, in a flash of insight she understood all her negative feelings. Fourteen years ago she'd turned away from him in a bid to make her own way in the world and to become more than she was. She'd been afraid that the force of his personality would overshadow her and cast all her potential into oblivion. The idea of marriage to him had terrified her. Now she recognized the source of the new emotion—the new fear—she kept feeling around him.

She was afraid of nothing so much as going through life without the opportunity to have all the things with Travis that he'd once offered her. The most precious of which had been his heart. Even now, though, if he were to offer her all of that, how could she accept with a career like hers?

And seeing Max Vance with his wife all ready to attend his regular church service gave her yet another uncomfortable feeling. She planned to spy on the man, and if at all possible do it in the sanctity of his own house and in the Lord's, as well. She was spying on Travis's hero—his father.

"Oh, Max. It's our Travis," she heard Lidia Vance call out as the older woman caught sight of them. His mother rushed ahead of Max, as fast as her short legs could carry her, leaving her husband lengthening his strides to keep up.

"I know who it is, dear," Max said, smiling fondly down at Lidia when he caught up. "Funny running into you here, son." Max Vance grinned sarcastically at Travis, then glanced at the sky.

Lidia playfully smacked Max's arm, drawing a wink from him. "Shh! Be good," she warned him.

Tricia could have sworn she heard Travis actually growl under his breath, which in turn made her wonder what the byplay between father and son had been about. And if she'd have the nerve later to ask. Tricia fought a grin. Feeling the way she did today, she just might.

She turned, smiling at Travis's grumbling. "Lidia, Max. How wonderful to see you."

"I'm assuming you talked our recalcitrant son into coming with you?" Max asked.

Tricia nodded and widened her smile, hoping to distract the Vances from their son's increasingly bad mood. "This is just like old times, isn't it?" Tricia said. "Can it be fourteen years ago both of you convinced me to attend services here with you?"

"And fourteen years ago you were both staying at the house with us," Lidia said. Then her eyes widened as if she had an idea. Tricia hoped it had something to do with dinner. "I know," his mother went on. "You should bring Tricia to dinner tonight. Oh, son, it would be like turning the clock back."

Travis's hand went to the base of his throat and he swallowed with obvious difficulty. His deep-set eyes seemed to darken with pain. "We don't get the chance to live things over. If we did, I couldn't pick *those* times, Mom. I just couldn't." His hand tightened on Tricia's as if trying to draw strength from her. "But we'll be over." He looked up at the stone facade of the church and dropped her hand. "Maybe we should go inside."

Lidia nodded but reached out and put her hand on Travis's forearm. "I'm glad to see you finally moving ahead. And don't you dare feel guilty. Natalie would want you to be happy."

Travis nodded and started moving toward the church alone. For a long moment Tricia watched, mulling over what Lidia had said. And what she hadn't. She hadn't mentioned what Allison would have wanted for Travis.

Chapter Eleven

Travis got halfway up the sidewalk before realizing he was rushing—actually rushing—and into church of all places. That was his first mistake. The second was leaving Tricia behind with his parents. Some new love interest he looked like.

So he stopped and turned. And found himself sucking a strangled breath. Tricia was even more devastating a sight at a second look. Why had he insisted she dress up? He'd been having enough trouble keeping his mind on this investigation before she showed up today looking like something out of a fashion magazine. Now he was having a hard time not tripping over his tongue.

When Tricia reached him, she stopped, tilting her head as if to ask, "What's up?" He held out his hand for her to take, not unmindful that the old, silent communication between them was back as if more than a decade and a mountain of hurt didn't stand between them.

"Sorry, my parents threw me with that dinner invitation even though we'd talked about it."

She shrugged. "It's okay. They throw me all the time. Don't get me wrong. I always liked them. I remembered this church after I came to the Lord. I only started coming to Good Shepherd after a friend told me you didn't attend anymore, but I knew your parents still did. I wanted to come here. I wanted to see them again. I guess I had them starring in my mind in my own version of *The Waltons*. It wasn't until I talked to your sister, Lucia, one day a few months ago that I found out everything wasn't always perfect for all of you with your father being away all the time."

"It was pretty near perfect except for Dad's…uh… job. Mom held it all together, though. She was the cement that bound us into a cohesive unit. Dad was happy so she was content. It's been better for her since he's been around more, though. Unfortunately, he seems restless to me. I'm not sure retirement agrees with him."

Tricia frowned as if the news disturbed her deeply. "Oh. That's too bad. Maybe you should spend more time with him."

"Maybe. Look, I didn't say this before and I should have. I don't go to Sunday dinners anymore. I haven't since right after the accident."

Her brow furrowed as she stared at him in clear disbelief. "Travis, that just doesn't make any sense. You have a wonderful family. That was a time you needed their support."

He nodded. "That was part of the problem. We were all grieving. Natalie was the only grandchild and she'd become almost the primary focus of everyone's attention for three years at those Sunday get-togethers. Someone was always grabbing the video camera and filming her doing ordinary things all kids do. There are probably fifty tapes of her hidden somewhere in that house. I went once and we were all just sitting there looking at each other not knowing what to say. I had to get out of there. I almost ran out of the house and I haven't gone back to a Sunday dinner since. I go other times—don't get me wrong. I'd never be able to stay away from there. But Sundays were family day. And I lost mine."

She sighed. "No. You lost *part* of yours. The rest is there waiting for you. You should have said something and I'd have tried to get us out of today. But maybe it's a good thing you didn't. Maybe it's time, Trav. Your mother's right. I don't imagine Natalie would want to see her daddy this unhappy and missing out on special times with his parents and brother and sister."

Travis looked around. "I'm just glad they didn't know I was coming. They'd probably have called ahead and ordered up a special sermon. Where did they go anyway? Did they say?"

"Your parents went in the side door to get a seat. Lidia said they'd meet us inside." Her gaze cut left and she grimaced slightly. "Uh-oh. More of your family at two o'clock. Sam, Jessica and her daughter. And Amy just saw us." Tricia grinned. "I can tell because her ponytails are bobbling. Are you…okay with Amy?"

Travis sighed. "This just gets better. I'm fine with Amy. How could I not be? She's a little love-bug. It's

Sam I'm not up for." He turned and saw Sam do a little double take, recover and change directions toward them. He wasn't sure which had Sam more surprised: his big brother at church or Tricia's new look.

Travis looked back at Tricia to do a quick review of that new look and once again found his mind emptying of all coherent thought. She was captivating. It was only now that she'd fixed herself up, that qualities she'd been hiding—ones he'd once been fallen in love with—had shown themselves again and he understood his own erratic emotions when he was near her.

The softer, nurturing Venus side of her, the one who worried about her friend, the one clearly worried for him had emerged and drew him, soothing his troubled spirit. But there was something more potent that drew him in the utterly irresistible way sailors were supposed to have been lured by the Sirens.

This working with the Valkyrie was fine. And connecting with Venus felt good. But it was the Siren in her that made him want to take hold of her and never let go.

A throat clearing dragged Travis's attention off Tricia. He forced himself to look and his gaze fell immediately onto his youngest brother's smirking face. When Sam opened his mouth, Travis knew a smart remark was about to follow and he just wasn't willing to go there. Not yet. So he pointed sharply at his brother and Sam closed his mouth then clearly thought better of caving in to blatant, if silent, intimidation. Once again he started to say something and Travis, finger still in the air added, "Aagh!"

So Sam shrugged, scooped Amy up, put his arm

around Jessica and quipped, "Come on, ladies. I'll have at the grump later. Remember, big brother, a Vance never forgets."

Amy giggled and peeked over Sam's shoulder, waving to him for all she was worth. Travis winked and blew her a kiss. After that, he and Tricia stood there awkwardly for a few more minutes, people passing on either side of them. Then music floated on the air and Tricia looked toward the front doors. "I think the service is starting. I hope you enjoy it. Pastor Gabriel is a dynamic speaker, but it's his messages of hope and forgiveness that's drawn so many new people."

She tilted her head. "Trav, you don't have to go it alone. God's waiting to help you move ahead. Maybe it's time to take the first step. No one's going to rush you to take the second till you're ready."

He eyed her, no longer thinking of her new look. "This didn't have a lot to do with the case, did it?"

She grinned but didn't answer. Instead she threaded her hand between his side and elbow, curling her fingers around it and coaxing him forward. It was the push he needed. He wasn't so self-delusional that he wasn't aware he'd been stalling.

Travis didn't know what he expected, but lightning didn't strike the bell tower as he entered. He smiled. He hadn't missed his father's pointed glance toward the heavens. No, the stars weren't falling from the sky, but he was still going inside a church. Maybe it was time. He looked at Tricia. Maybe it was time for a lot of things.

Memories from his formative years assailed him as

the familiar smell—flowers, lemon oil and brewing coffee—hit his senses. The scents of Good Shepherd
Church. The pastor leading the worship had changed.
The members of the congregation had changed. Even
the style of music—his brother playing the keyboard
and singing a hymn he'd never heard—had changed.
But the foundation of it all hadn't.

And it felt like coming home.

He'd heard his parents and brother and sister talk
about Pastor Gabriel Dawson but the man was even
more charismatic in person than they'd said. A former
marine, he'd recently married Susan Carter, the direc-
tor of Galilee Women's Shelter. Just as Sam had ac-
quired an instant family through his marriage to
Jessica, Gabriel Dawson had gained Susan's twins as
daughters. The twins now sat as part of a circle of
children at the foot of the pulpit, flanking Amy, each
holding one of her hands. They both leaned toward
Amy, and Travis's three-year-old niece let out a quiet
giggle.

Travis was surprised to see his niece out of Jessica
or Sam's immediate care. Maybe they were a little less
nervous now. After Amy'd been kidnapped by a child-
care worker at the shelter back in August, neither of
them let the kid out of their sight for a moment when
she was in their care—not even on their short weekend
honeymoon. He grinned as his eyes settled on Sam who
was watching Amy like a hawk—or a mother hen.

Tricia took Travis's arm, calling him back to the service and gesturing for him to sit. He was so out of prac-

tice, someone would think his parents hadn't raised him in the church at all.

"Today we've been asked to offer a special prayer. Three years ago today Maxwell and Lidia Vance's son Peter left on a business trip. He's been out of touch with the family since. Three years, Lord, is a long time for us mere mortals...."

Travis's mind spun off on a tangent causing him to miss the rest of the pastor's prayer. Three years? Had it really been three years that Peter had been gone? It didn't seem possible. He glanced around at the congregation, heads all bowed in prayer for Peter. A lot of these people had probably given his brother up for dead. Travis hadn't for one moment felt that way. The breakup of his marriage had hit Peter harder than he'd let on. He'd be back when he was ready. But three years! Where did the time go?

"One Peter 5, verses 6 and 7," Pastor Gabriel, said, catapulting Travis back to the present with the sound of his brother's name. "'Therefore humble yourselves under the mighty hand of God, that He may exalt you in due time, casting all your care upon Him, for He cares for you.'"

Okay, now that's weird. Travis felt as if the Lord had just spoken to him in his brother's name. He thought about his feelings about God. He'd begun this last decade angry at Him for the accident but now Travis realized it had become a habit. The anger was gone. And in its place sat a void where God had once lived. A void he needed filled.

Allison hadn't been interested in the message of the church but she'd gone, treating it like a club and the service as if it were the business portion of a weekly meeting. To her, church was something one did. An experience you gave a child, and for Natalie she'd have done anything. She might have been spoiled and selfish about what she wanted in life but she'd loved Natalie.

To Travis, church was God and God had been a refuge from the day in and day out struggles on the streets. God was strength to face another day. God was hope of a better tomorrow. And He meant there was an eternity of joy ahead when there were no more tomorrows.

Why was I so angry at You, Lord? Bad things happen. I saw it in my job. Maybe I thought I should be a special case. That You should have just reached down and picked the boat up and out of danger. I guess You were with me for so long I figured You ought to share some of the blame I deserved. I'm sorry. I just missed her so much. She was just a little kid with so much living to do. That's what I still don't understand.

"Today we're looking at Luke 12, verses 6 and 7." Travis heard the pastor's dynamic voice calling him back to the service. "'Are not five sparrows sold for two copper coins?'" Gabriel Dawson read. "'And not one of them is forgotten before God. But the very hairs of your head are all numbered.'"

The pastor looked up from the Bible and looked around. "The Father loves us and *knows* us. Intimately. That's what Luke tells us Jesus said. What a beautiful message He came to us with. Does that mean we won't live with trial and pain and loss? No, it does not. Don't listen if someone tries to tell you that. Because the Father knows more than just the number of hairs on our heads. He knows the number of days you and you and you will live." He pointed to three random people.

"Each of us leaves someone behind to mourn. But His message isn't about doom and gloom. It's full of hope, don't you see? Because Jesus also left this earth to go and prepare a place for us. A better place for you and you and you," he said pointing to the same people he had before. "Let's face facts, here. We don't mourn for the ones who've gone on. We mourn for *us*. That's the selfish human part of us weeping at the gravesides of this earth. We're the ones in pain. Feeling loss and lost. Alone with our hearts saddened and empty of our loved ones' love and companionship. Why don't we smile at funerals? Why, oh why, don't we praise Him for taking another soul into eternal bliss?"

Because I was only thinking about me, Lord, Travis thought. *I never tried to comfort Mom or Dad, did I? They lost Natalie, too. I only saw me and my anguish. I didn't for one second think that Natalie was with You in perfect happiness. Bad things happen and You make them as right as You can without forcing even one of us fools down here to Your will.*

I'm sorry, Lord. I'm so sorry for all the years I spoke against You to my family. For wallowing in all of this. Please settle my heart about the accident. Please take away my anger at Allison and my grief over the child I had and lost. When Allison told me about her, You know how I felt. Maybe I was afraid this was a punishment for not wanting our baby at first. But I know You'd never do that. You aren't about punishing us when we've repented. And I did. But I sure snatched it back and rolled myself up in it, didn't I? I'm sorry for that, too.

He sighed and continued a prayer long overdue. *So take my guilt and I promise not to hold on to it anymore. I loved my baby girl and I tried to love Allison. I'd never have left her or been unfaithful, and You know that.* Travis felt Tricia's presence next to him and added, *And could You tell me what to do about Tricia? She must be back in my life for a reason. If it's love, then help us both get past the past. Help us forgive each other. And help me see what it was I did back then to push her away so I don't do it again.*

A hand on his sleeve and a pretty monogrammed handkerchief pressed into his hand brought him back once again to the church home of his childhood. His mother smiled softly and patted his arm. "Welcome home, son," she whispered. As he wiped away the cleansing tears he hadn't realized he'd shed, he knew his mother was right. He was home again where he belonged. Life wasn't perfect but it was life and it was time he started to live it. Time to cut the ties of the past.

Time to unlock one more door.

He glanced at Tricia. And time he overcame one more obstacle in his heart. They had to talk. He had to explain about his marriage and he had to ask what he'd done to make her break up with him. And if it had been all about her, even if there was no hope for them, he had to forgive her.

Chapter Twelve

Tricia stepped aside as Travis's family gathered around him at the end of the service. When Pastor Gabriel began his message, it had sounded made to order for Travis and what he'd been through. Still, she'd been surprised when he answered Pastor Gabriel's altar call. She smiled. And there'd been no family conspiracy with the pastor about the topic he chose. She was the only one who knew— and even she hadn't known for sure—that Travis was coming. The Lord worked in this world in small quiet ways, but He surely did work.

A terrible sadness came over her. Maybe ge... Travis here really was the only reason sh... brought back into his life. She couldn't regre... found his way back to the Lord, but she ... wanted that to be the only reason she'd run i... in that shadowed alley.

So much had happened in such a short time. Could it really have been only a week ago that Travis burst into her life and turned it upside down? She glanced at him

as a smile broke across his face over some teasing remark his father made.

Travis was smiling. Really smiling. All the way to his
beautiful eyes. She guessed hers wasn't the only life
turned upside down this past week.

It seemed inconceivable that she could feel all she did
for Travis after the way he'd hurt her—the way he'd
turned to Allison after refusing to give Tricia the time
she'd needed. She'd forgiven him long ago but she was
surprised that the hurt still lingered. Maybe no one ever
got over their first love until they'd loved someone else.
Maybe that was her problem. After Travis, she'd closed
off that side of her, too afraid to love after losing it the
way she had. For the reason she had.

What Travis hadn't understood, and maybe back then
neither had she, was that love had always hurt and disappointed her. More damage than she'd realized had been
done to her soul by those early years with her parents and
the subsequent fractured and loveless years of her later
childhood after being taken away from them. She'd
moved from foster home to foster home, never belonging
anywhere, cared for by people pretending love when in
fact her care had been nothing but a job to most of them.

Of course she'd still been too ashamed to tell any of
her new friends the depths from which she'd climbed by
freshman year of college. She'd arrived at school and had
told herself it was all behind her. She was a new person.
But she'd spent every waking moment waiting—just
waiting—for life to kick her in the teeth. It finally did
the night Travis walked away from her. She'd expected

to be hurt because she hadn't been a new person at all. And she didn't become one until she found the Lord.

Someone pitched a penny into her lap from the pew in front of her, dragging Tricia back to the now-silent church. She picked it up then looked up into eyes as bright and green as the trees of summer back in Pennsylvania. Travis's eyes.

He pointed to the penny. "It's...uh...for those deep thoughts. I'll warn you though, I think you'd be selling out cheap. They looked pretty important."

"They were...once. But no more." She smiled, gently. "My life's an open book these days."

"Good. Because I think we need to talk."

She looked around at the empty church. She really had been deep in thought. "Where did your family go?"

"Mom and Dad and the rest of the Vance clan went over to the church hall. Something about punch and cookies. I took a pass and promised we'd be over to their house by three. I told them there were some things I wanted to clear up with you first. Maybe we could take a walk in the Garden of the Gods."

"Sounds perfect," she said, but as she gathered her things, she worried about what he wanted to talk about. On the way to the garden, she caught him up on the news about Elliott Harrison's condition, then they fell into a silence she was afraid to break.

Travis parked and headed toward Siamese Twins Trail. It was one of her favorite trails and one he'd taken her on fifteen years ago when she'd visited his hometown for a weekend during a holiday break. It was an easy half-mile-long trail that looped back to the start-ing point.

The clear blue sky shone over the distant vista of the snow-covered summit of Pikes Peak. Because of the natural window of the twin rocks, the trail offered a unique view of the mountain and the gorgeous fall fo-liage. In continued silence, they stood for a while en-joying it before Tricia's nerves stretched to their limit.

"What did you want to talk about?" she asked.

He blinked. "I'm sorry. I guess I'm having a little trouble getting started. The past—I wanted to see if we could put it to rest."

"I did that a long time ago, Travis. At least I tried to."

He sighed. "How could you when I've given you such a hard time since we met up again?"

"You had your reasons. I've dealt with worse in my life. Believe me."

"I'd still like to apologize for being such a grump."

She grinned, trying to feign surprise. "Have you been grumpy? I hadn't noticed."

He shot her a wry grin. "Right. And you didn't storm out of the O Club because of it."

"I never storm."

His grin widened as he looked away, back at the glo-rious scene, then up the trail. Gesturing ahead, he said, "Of course not. I must be mistaken." She loved hearing the smile in his voice again. They walked in silence.

"er walk Ridge Trail?" Travis asked when they got k to their starting point.

Ridge Trail was another short half mile circling path

with only a one-hundred-foot rise and was one of the easier trails. A few minutes in, at a particularly spectacular view, Travis stopped and sighed. "Pull up a rock, would you?"

She nodded and boosted herself onto a rock. The path was billed as giving the feeling of being among the rocks and it lived up to its press. She felt secluded and safe among God's creation until Travis stood in front of her at nearly eye level and said, "I need to tell you what happened."

It seemed his stalling was over. "Happened?" she asked, with her heart suddenly thundering and truly no clue of what was to come.

"After we had that fight a few weeks before I graduated."

"Travis, you don't have to—"

He held up his hand. "Yes, I do, or we'll never get by it. You *do* want to try to get past it, don't you? Tell me I'm not the only one feeling this pull between us." He waited a beat for her to protest then went on, her silence all the confirmation he seemed to need. And since she was suddenly speechless it was a good thing.

"That's something I think we should explore," he concluded, "but first I know we have to settle what happened. Since you were pretty up-front about turning me down, I thought I should explain what happened between Allison and me."

She shrugged, hoping to look careless, but she didn't feel at all indifferent. "You started dating someone willing to give you what I couldn't. What's to explain?"

He winced. "I didn't start seeing her. We'd never even had a real date when I married her."

Tricia could only stare. *Okay. That wasn't on her list of guesses.* "I admit to being fascinated," she quipped.

"I went back to your place about two hours after I stormed away from you. I'd had a couple of drinks." Again he winced. "Okay, more than a couple."

"You don't drink."

He sighed. "Unfortunately, I did that night. Allison wouldn't let me in to see you. She said you were too upset to put up with me drunk. She offered to mediate. We went to Cavanaugh's to talk. I had several more beers and so did she." He shook his head. Closing his eyes he pivoted and leaned on the rock next to her legs. "We ended up at my place, Trish. Until the next morning. I woke up and she was cheerfully making breakfast. She was wearing my shirt. Her clothes were everywhere."

Tricia's heart sank. She could almost imagine the scene. This was worse than she'd thought. Travis never drank. Something was wrong with this story but she was too shaken to put her finger on what. "You slept with her?"

"Apparently. Not that I remember, even to this day. After that I was too ashamed to come near you. I'd waited for you and…I couldn't face you, so I stayed away. Avoided you. Two days before graduation I went to your place again to confess and to try to find out if there was hope for us. I still didn't know what I'd done to make you turn down my proposal. Allison was there instead."

"Oh? And you realized she was the one you wanted?"

He shook his head. "And she had news. She said she was pregnant. I felt like my heart had exploded. There was only one solution. My parents were there for graduation and I told them I was going to marry her but not why. They were shocked, disappointed. They liked you." He crossed his arms and pursed his lips. "I'd never disappointed them before."

Light dawned. Allison hadn't spent that night with him. And she hadn't been pregnant. Roommates knew that sort of thing. But should she tell him? Allison was dead after all. Then she realized he must have found out since there hadn't been a baby. "How long did she lie?"

He shook his head, still not looking at her. A bird fluttered out of the nearby brush breaking the deadly silence momentarily. "She told me when she was really pregnant with Natalie. She claimed it was all a mistake made at the clinic she'd gone to in Philadelphia. I didn't believe her. I wanted to, but…" He sighed and ran a restless hand through his hair. Then his lips thinned. "She'd wanted marriage and she got it."

"No. She wanted *you*. And I handed you over to her. I came home the night we argued about getting married and cried on her shoulder. I told her all about your proposal—that you wanted a wife and children more than you wanted to be with me."

He did look at her then, hitching his hip up onto the rock as he turned to face her. "Did I say it all that badly?"

She shrugged. "You wouldn't wait. I told you I wasn't ready to marry you and you wouldn't wait."

"You weren't ready to marry *me*," he pointed out.

"Yes, *you*. I'd never have considered marrying anyone else. I still haven't, have I?"

His one dark brow arched, furrowing his brow, clearly for the first time considering what her single state might mean.

She touched his shoulder. "I'll get to me and why that was in a little while. Right now, let's sort out Allison." He nodded and she went on. "She was spoiled. She got whatever she wanted. And she wanted you. I had you but that didn't stop her. Several times through the year she'd made joking references to thinking seriously about working her wiles on you because you were— how did she put it?—an unpolished gem."

Tricia paused. It was uncomfortable telling him these things about Allison when she was not around to defend herself. But truth was truth. She sighed and went on. "I don't know what happened between the two of you that night but she was in our apartment at six that morning then she rushed out. And she wasn't pregnant right before your graduation. Roommates know those things, Trav."

He shook his head and crossed his arms. "She worked awfully hard to wind up miserable."

What an odd thing for him to say. Or maybe they hadn't been deliriously happy. Maybe Allison had lied about that, too. "After I learned you two got married, I applied and got into the Air Force Academy here in Colorado Springs. You must have figured that out by now. I had to get away from campus. I thought Allison would continue on there and that you'd start out your career there. Probably even stay there to be near her family. They doted on her but I guess you found that out."

"Oh…yeah." He squinted a bit, deep in thought. "But what does all that have to do with anything other than explaining why you applied to the Air Force? I knew you were in the Air Force. My family started ragging me about you when you showed up at Good Shepherd. What surprised me when we met up Monday was that you're an Air Force investigator. When I heard you were in the Air Force and stationed here, I assumed you were some sort of technician or a secretary."

He shook his head. "How could it have only been Monday?" he said, clearly sharing her wonder at the scope of the past week and turned more fully to face her. "I never knew what happened to you," he whispered, and touched her cheek. "I guess I could have found out, but I didn't have a right to."

He dropped his hand to his thigh when she said, "No, you didn't." She saw him wince but kept on. She had things to say, too. "Allison had already made sure that you didn't. Travis, I ran into her at a drugstore in Manitou Springs in December of that year. I didn't want to hear about how happy you were so I avoided Colorado Springs where I thought I might run into your parents. That's why I was up shopping in Manitou Springs in the first place. But I heard anyway. From Allison. And with a vengeance."

It hurt to talk about that day. Waves of pain and remembered embarrassment rolled over Tricia. Were she not wearing a skirt she'd have hugged her knees to her chest. She used to sit that way as a girl, trying to shrink so no one would notice her. Instead she slid to the ground and forced herself to stand in front of him, holding his gaze. She was no longer the coward she'd been. "She was furious that I was living so nearby. She accused me of wanting to break up your marriage. According to her, she was giving you everything you wanted. Everything I'd refused to."

Tricia let out an unladylike snort and used it as an excuse to look away as she crossed her arms. Maybe she was still just a little defensive after all. "I already knew that. She was visibly pregnant so it was obvious you two had started the family I was afraid to give you. She said you two were as deliriously happy together as she'd been sure you would be. And she thanked me for handing her the key to your heart—the knowledge that you wanted marriage and children and that I couldn't give you them."

"I wanted marriage to *you*." The anger in his voice drew her eyes back to Travis's. He pushed himself upright and looked down at her. "Why didn't you want it with *me?*"

Tricia backed away a step or two and leaned back against the rock that now stood directly behind her. "Travis, you were *so much!* You'd *had* so much! I'd never had anything."

His lips thinned. "Money? This was about money?"

"It was about *love!* Or the lack of it," she finished in a quieter contemplative tone.

"I loved you," he protested angrily. "Your rejection almost tore my heart out."

She searched his gaze, praying for understanding. "You said you loved me, but I kept expecting love to kick me in the teeth. Then it finally did when you wouldn't wait for me. I should have turned you down differently. I should have explained why first, then maybe you would have understood. As it was, you just walked away."

"I'm not going anywhere now," he promised.

Was this a second chance or were they just clearing the air? What had he said? *Tell me I'm not the only one feeling this pull between us.*

This time she forced herself to hold his gaze. "Don't be so sure. Travis, my father was a two-bit drug dealer, a thief and a user. He was also an abuser who beat my mother—and me if she wasn't there. The police took me away from them and put me in foster care when I was eight. I'd called the cops when he was beating my mother. She wasn't much but she did try to protect me— when she was sober, that is."

"I thought you lived with her when she died."

She nodded. "I only went to live with her again when I was seventeen. My father died of a drug overdose a year earlier. She'd finally cleaned herself up but not for me. With his influence gone, she woke up to where she was and where she was headed. When you met me, I wasn't going to school on her life insurance money. There was no life insurance. She was hit by a car and killed on her way home from work one night. My mother cleaned toilets in a center city office building. That kind of work was all there was for someone with her history. You knew I was going to school on the mayor's scholarship. And that it paid my board and books, too. And that the part-time job I had covered spending money. But you didn't know I had nowhere to go in summer."

"Why keep that a secret?"

She refused to look away. "Shame. You don't know what it's like to be embarrassed about where you come from. About the substance of who you are. You think those students would have accepted me? At an Ivy League college?"

He stepped closer. Within touching distance. "I would have."

Knowing *that* had allowed her to forgive him for the most part, even in absentia. She put her hand on his shoulder. "Oh, Travis. I know that now. But this was then and I was only eighteen when I met you. When you asked me to marry you, I still had to prove I could make it on my own at twenty. That I could be someone other than your wife. Or I'd never have been the best me I could be. If I'd taken the easy way out and said yes, I'd have lived in your shadow. I'd have been your wife but I would have had no idea who *I* was. I'd spent most of my life trying not to make waves, hiding in plain sight from everyone just to buy two more weeks in a good school or at a clean house. I was afraid no one would see me next to you, that I'd disappear altogether." With conviction she added, "And I would have, Travis. I would have because I wasn't anyone yet."

He took a deep breath and gathered the hand she'd

laid on his shoulder in his. "I know. I already realized I'd have held you back and that I was too blinded by what I wanted out of life to be what you needed. I didn't give you a chance to explain. I just went out, got drunk and destroyed my life and Allison's and eventually Natalie's. And I did to you what Allison did to me. I didn't think about what you needed. I guess I was as bad for you as she was for me."

Tricia frowned. "I don't understand."

"She lied to you that day you met her," he said on a deep sigh. "We weren't happy. She could never forget that she'd been second. My wife by default, she called herself. I swear I never did anything to make her feel that way, but she knew I was always doing what I thought I should. Because I didn't feel anything for her other than as the mother of my child. I did love her for that. She was a good mother. And she tried to be a good wife—at first. She may have even believed we were happy but I doubt it."

He pivoted and leaned next to her again. Still holding her hand, he laced their fingers together and went on. "After Natalie was born, Allison started trying to make me change who I was. What was it you said? She saw me as some dull stone just waiting to be polished up and made into something more than I was. I was just a cop and that wasn't enough for her. She wasn't just on vacation at her parents' lakefront property when they were all killed in the accident. She was deciding if she would leave me because I wouldn't quit the force. I should have given in, but I didn't think she'd really do it. I didn't think she'd admit defeat to the parents. I took a risk and Natalie lost her life."

Tricia wanted to say something but his grief was so palpable. But maybe it wasn't all grief. Maybe there was a good portion of guilt. And that just wasn't fair.

Then he confirmed her instincts. "Everyone thought it was grief that kept me from moving ahead, but it was guilt more than anything else," he admitted. "If I'd given in to Allison's demands, they'd be alive today."

Tricia pushed off the rock, but Travis held tight to her hand as she turned to face him. No way was she letting this go on. "Allison knew your plans. Everyone knew you were going into law enforcement. It was your major. You were born to be a cop. You can't imagine how shocked I was that you aren't anymore."

Travis pursed his lips and nodded, tugging her a step closer into the V of his legs. "Today I realized that if they'd stayed home, something else might have happened to them. The point is, I can't go on this way, half-alive. Half-buried with them. It isn't the life the Lord wants for me." He cupped her cheek. "It isn't the life *I* want for me." He stood, the look in his eyes intense and purposeful. "And I'm thinking it isn't the life you wanted for me or you wouldn't have dragged me to Good Shepherd. What I want is you and what we had."

And then he kissed her.

Chapter Thirteen

Trish moaned, her arms encircling his neck as he pulled her against him. He'd meant it to be a sweet kiss. Sweet as the smell of the vanilla perfume she wore. A first-time kiss. Gentle as the breeze that stirred the air. He didn't know by what miracle she was responding to him instead of clawing his eyes out or punching him in the gut the way she had last time, but he wasn't complaining. Because fighting him would definitely be more like the new Patricia Streeter than this knee-weakening response he'd gotten. Travis no longer cared about the changes in her. In fact, he was smart enough to realize that the girl from his past hadn't been half the woman the person in his arms was.

She was more of a woman, to be sure. The feel of her so near set his heart pounding, and that was exactly why he put her away from him—only to find himself held captive by the look in her deep chocolate eyes. And that look gave him all the courage he needed to ask his next question.

"What I want to know is what you want to do about us," he breathed, then all but collapsed against the rock formation behind him.

She shook her head, looking as dazed as he felt. "Us." She blinked a little owlishly. "It's been a week, Travis. Seven days since you exploded back into my life."

"Actually," he said, hoping to lighten the moment, "since you're the one who ran into me, I'd say you exploded into mine. At least that's how it feels from this side."

"Right." She nodded once sharply. "And I feel as if the collision knocked my life off track. I knew what I wanted when I got up last Monday morning. I wanted to get the people responsible for Ian Kelly's death. I wanted my promotion."

"And now? You don't want those things? You want something else? Something different?"

She shook her head and looked away. "I still want those things, but I think I want more, too. I don't know how that can happen so, in a way, I'm afraid to think about it. I don't know which way is up anymore," she confessed, her hand going to her forehead as if she, too, felt the dizzying kind of mental vertigo he did. She looked back, her eyes imploring. "I've been alone a long time, Trav. And you hurt me so desperately. One day I was hoping against hope that you were real and that your love wasn't going to disappoint me the way love always had before. Then you wouldn't listen to what I was trying so badly to say. I walked around like a zombie for weeks, hoping you'd come to me ready to listen. Finally Joanne Barber knocked on the door, walked into Allison's room and opened the closet. It was empty and she told me where Allison had gone—off to marry you. Joanne wasn't trying to be cruel. She was trying to wake me up. If she'd stuck a knife in my heart, it couldn't have hurt or shocked me more. Now fourteen years later here you are. And, Trav, you aren't easy.

"Friday night I wanted to kick you so hard your eyes would've bulged for a week. Yesterday I decided to knock your socks off instead." She gestured to her new look.

He grinned. "Consider them knocked."

She punched his arm in frustration. "You make me crazy!" More quietly she said, "You make me scared you'll hurt me again. I don't like being afraid. That isn't me anymore." She shook her head in clear frustration. "Oh! I don't know what I feel anymore."

He reached out and traced her jaw with a fingertip. "Maybe that's enough for now. Maybe we should just go on the way we were and see where the feelings and fears take us. I'm a little unsure, too. A guy doesn't get over having his proposal turned down overnight, you know. We have fragile egos."

She grinned as he'd hoped she would. "Fourteen years?"

He had to smile. She'd stepped right into this one. "A Vance never forgets," he said, repeating the old family motto to her as he often had in college.

She rolled her eyes and looked pointedly at her watch. "Did you forget what time you told your parents we'd be there?"

He glanced at her wrist. "Oops. Guess we'd better get a move on." He pushed to his feet and looped his arm around her shoulders, hugging her to his side. "We can go by and talk to Elliott Harrison first if you want."

He took her chin and tipped it up just a bit. In heels she still wasn't quite as tall as he was and he wanted her to really hear what he had to say. Wanted to be sure she understood. She had to learn to level with him on all fronts or they'd never get beyond her childhood or his adult mistakes.

"We can't keep secrets from each other, Trish. My dad always says secrets and half-truths find a way of coming back to bite you. That's what destroyed us before. If you'd told me about your childhood, I'd have understood you better and I might not have gotten so mad. If I'd come to you the next day and told you what I thought had happened with Allison the night before, you'd have set me straight about where she really spent the night. Maybe we'd have been together all these years. Maybe not. But I doubt they'd stand between us like some great big chasm we still have to learn to cross."

She winced and nodded, a look of guilt shadowing her pretty eyes. "Let's go right to your parents'. We can go see Elliott this evening. His parents will be there with him most of the day."

Travis nodded, sorry she so clearly blamed herself that Elliott was in the hospital, but now they at least knew he'd live.

* * *

Sunday dinner at the Vances' big old Dutch Colonial home was a culinary experience in homemade Italian cuisine. It was also a free-for-all basketball game, a loud and boisterous debate on everything from what chance the Rockies had of getting into the next World Series to presidential politics. Opinions on all subjects were varied and hotly contested. It was all about family and exactly as she remembered it.

Wonderful.

This feeling of hearth and home was something she'd never had. And she realized it was something she wanted but would never have as long as she stayed in the Air Force, because her job took her too many places for too short an amount of time. Whether it was an even trade she was not yet sure. But at that moment the Air Force was losing.

Max Vance, having retired from the vagabond life of military service, certainly seemed relaxed and happy in the midst of his big family. And less like a suspect than ever. That allowed her to relax for the first time since seeing him with General Hadley. She'd nearly shouted out the truth at the Garden of the Gods when Travis referred to his father's advice on keeping secrets.

Talk about secrets and half-truths tearing them apart!

She was spying on his father—at home and at church. She'd started out using Travis to get close to the man because she suspected Travis's hero of masterminding serious crimes. If she were forced to have his father arrested, any chance they had would disappear in a flash.

But now it looked as if it would be okay. Until she noticed both Max and Travis missing. Thinking the worst—that Travis was off with his father for a little private talk about the investigation—she went in search of them.

Fortunately, they weren't together.

Unfortunately, she found Max in his office on the phone. Before she could make her presence known, she heard Max say, "Okay. So fifty kilos are due Sunday? Late?" He was quiet for a long time then said, "Good luck. Go careful out there."

Hearing the receiver drop into the cradle, Tricia stepped quickly backward before she was seen. Then just as she started to retrace her steps, Lidia's voice floated up the hall toward her. The stairs were to her left so Tricia quickly took them. With any luck she'd find Travis up there and could make an excuse to leave. She needed to think about what she'd heard and all the different interpretations it could have. Unfortunately, she couldn't come up with one that had Max starring as anything other than the villain of the piece.

A childish giggle came from a bedroom and washed over her as she moved into the upstairs hall. Confused she stopped and listened. It couldn't be Amy. Sam's stepdaughter had fallen asleep in his arms and he'd laid her on the sofa in Max's study. It was one of the reasons the conversation she'd just overheard so chilled her. Such dirty work done in the presence of such innocence. It made her nauseous just to think about all the implications. The main one was that it looked as if the entire Vance family was in for a world of hurt.

Yet another giggle and Travis's laughter, bright and free drifted from a bedroom two doors up the hall, beckoning her. But it wasn't Amy she'd heard. It was little Natalie and her adoring father's laughter emanating from a TV screen. Travis sat in a club chair, his gaze locked on the screen. Unsure if she should intrude, she also couldn't seem to drag herself away, to leave him alone with that poignant look of love and pride on his face. Travis was on the road to recovery but she was sure he still had some rocky spots to negotiate.

So she slid into the room and settled on the arm of his chair. When he reached for her hand, she took it and dropped her other arm across his shoulders, just watching the video with him. There was a wading pool, a hose and adults willing to be squirted. And so much pure innocent fun it was uplifting and heartbreaking at the same time.

The only one dry when the tape ran out had been Natalie. Travis paused the film on the last fame as he got a big smacking kiss from the curly-haired child in his arms.

"No wonder you felt her loss so deeply. She was a sweetheart, Travis." Tricia ran her fingers through his hair. "She had your black hair."

He shook his head, staring at the TV. "Allison had black hair, too."

She pointed to the screen, then ruffled his perpetually messy hair. "But Natalie's was like yours."

He chuckled. It was a slightly rusty sound but it sounded wonderful. Another sign he was finally healing. "Yeah. I guess so. It was all over the place, huh?

Allison gave up controlling it and went with containment. She was a good mother. I loved Natalie so I had to love Allison for that."

Allison was there, frozen in time in the background, soaking wet and laughing, love for her family in her eyes. "And I think she loved you both. Look at the way she's looking at you two."

"I should have watched these before. I should have remembered Natalie like *this,* not the way she looked at the funeral in the coffin. So still and silent. She didn't even hold still when she was asleep. She was always out of the covers. She was so happy all the time. And…she still is." He pointed to the screen. "That's what I want to think of when I think of my child." He touched the base of his throat. "There's something I need to do. Would you mind running by my house with me before we go to the hospital?"

"That's fine," she said, remembering the conversation she'd overheard while on the hunt for Travis. She didn't want to stay around Maxwell Vance a second longer than necessary. And she certainly didn't want to think about how much what his father was doing was going to break Travis's already-damaged heart.

It took forty minutes to free themselves from the family and drive up to Manitou Springs. Travis seemed to be walking in a fog by then, hardly paying Cody any mind at all. He just dropped his keys on the breakfast bar, walked through the main living area that he used as an office space then went down the hall toward the bedrooms.

Unsure if he meant for her to follow, Tricia hung back. But a beat later, when she heard the distinctive sound of a lock snicking open, curiosity got the better of her and she followed. Travis stood in the doorway of the room she'd assumed all along had been Natalie's.

She'd been right.

Ballet clearly had been Allison's inspiration and pink was the major color in the palette. The walls were a pale pink that was almost white. About three quarters of the way up the walls ran a border of pink satin toe shoes tied up with trailing ribbons that meandered along a navy blue matte background. Above the border she'd painted a sky full of fluffy clouds—the occasional fairy wearing toe shoes peeked down at the room from over a cloud.

"We'd just finished this," Travis said. "It was her big girl room. She picked out everything."

"Not Allison?"

He shook his head and grinned, picking up a bank that looked like a pair of slippers. "Natalie was the idea girl on this. We took her to see *The Nutcracker* and she decided she was going to be a world-famous ballerina. She said she wanted to fly the way Clara had. Allison painted the sky and the fairies. Sugarplum fairies. Natalie controlled the placement."

His mouth kicked up into a proud smile. "Three years old. She was so so smart. I think she was smarter than the adults in her world. We spent hours together in here making this perfect. I really thought we were going to be all right."

He shook his head in disgust, walked to a miniature dressing table and opened a small jewelry box that sat there. A dancer in a tutu danced as the music box started playing. Sounds of *The Nutcracker* filled the room.

"Oh, God," he said, and sank cross-legged to the floor. "Ten years," he said, a sob in his voice. "She's been waiting to dance for ten years."

"You never come in here, do you?"

He shook his head and took a deep breath. "I make sure Mrs. Timothy can get in to keep it clean. Then I lock it away. What did I think that was going to accomplish?"

She sat in the little chair. The music box still played. The ballerina still danced. "You were just putting this off till you could handle it. That's all."

He pursed his lips and nodded, continuing to stare at the little ballerina doing her dance until the music box finally wound down. When it did, he exhaled as if steeling himself. Then he reached up and unsnapped the catch on the chain around his neck. Looping it around his hand Travis dangled a tiny ring in the air for a second then draped it over his fist. He stared down at it. "I gave her this for her third birthday." He sighed. "She didn't wear it all that long. I've worn it a whole lot longer." He made a disgusted sound. "She'd be so mad at me for this." His lower lip trembled. "You didn't walk around being grumpy around her.

"I'd come home all riled up from something that had happened on the job and she'd put those chubby little fists on her hips and say, 'Daddy, smile. Your face won't break!'"

Tricia chuckled. "She picked that up from your mother."

"She picked up on everything we said. I accidentally taught her her first and last swear word when she was eighteen months old. I thought—" his voice broke "—my mother would kill me."

"Why are we in here, Trav?"

He looked up at her, those green eyes swimming with tears. "Because it's time to say goodbye." He kissed the ring. "Bye, angel face," he whispered, then twined the chain around the feet of the little ballerina that had finally ended her dance after a long ten-year wait. He closed the lid, and cried.

Chapter Fourteen

Later that night, Tricia walked out of ICU discouraged and upset. She nodded to the guard outside Elliott's little glass-enclosed room and went to find Travis. The usually teeming halls of Vance Memorial were quiet except for the plaintive sound of Elliott's baby crying in the ICU waiting room. Teddy had clearly picked up on his grandparents' anxiety.

She found Travis at the end of the hall to ICU, staring out of a window toward the mountains. He turned and held out his arms, clearly keying in on her expression. "He still can't remember anything?"

Grateful for the support, she walked into his embrace and laid her head on his shoulder. It felt so good to be held again by him, she found herself sighing. "Not a thing," she whispered. "It's hard to see him so upset about this arrest thing and not tell him it's okay. His blood pressure's through the roof for a guy his age. It's making the effect of the concussion worse across the board."

"Then Fielding's going to have to authorize telling him. That's all there is to it."

"I know." She stepped out of his arms, hitched a hip onto the deep windowsill and leaned back against the frame. "Besides, from here he'd go to the stockade. That just can't be safe."

Travis looked around, his eyes narrowed as if he saw potential assassins around every corner. "I'm not so sure this is the best place to keep someone safe, either. Two separate attempts were made on Adam while he was at Memorial recovering. Kate Montgomery was snatched from the parking garage. I'm working on a security plan for the hospital, but nothing's been implemented, so keeping him safe here is still a security nightmare. And keeping him safe in custody on the base would be even worse than this. We're already pretty sure someone on the base can't be trusted. To top that off, this cartel has deep enough pockets to pay for a hit nearly anywhere. So, I've been thinking. It might be better if Elliott were dead."

She jumped to her feet. Had he gone around the bend? "Travis!"

Travis laughed at Tricia's outrage. "Calm down and hear me out," he told her as he looped his arm around her shoulders and pulled her against his side. He started them walking farther away from ICU. Farther away from Teddy Harrison's fretful wailing. "If Elliott were dead, he'd be out of danger and the case wouldn't be compromised with the need for premature arrests to keep him safe. So why don't we just *say* he died?"

"Because we don't know who Ian confided in. The red tape surrounding any death is pretty extensive but it's worse with the military. There may be somebody on base who would realize Elliott isn't dead if all the *i*'s aren't dotted and the *t*'s crossed."

She had a point so his mind moved to the next possible solution. It was a crazy idea but… "Then we stage his death and his parents go back to Phoenix and bury a box of rocks in a private funeral. We stash your pal somewhere safe. I can get Jake Montgomery to use his FBI connections to help with that."

He walked them into a solarium down the hall and around the corner from the ICU family room and Harrison's parents. The bug detection device in his pocket didn't vibrate, telling him the room was safe. He motioned to a couple of chairs in the empty room and continued with his admittedly insane plan. "The Bucs wouldn't feel threatened anymore that at any moment he might remember who tried to kill him. Everybody's happy. The only problem I see is his parents. I don't see how we could lie to them about their son's death, but I'm not sure they could pull it off convincingly."

Tricia grinned. "Travis, this is brilliant. Really brilliant. And I don't think the Harrisons would be a problem. They're a lot tougher than they look. He was a Green Beret. She was an Army nurse. They met in Vietnam when Mr. Harrison was injured and brought into her aid station. I think they could do it, especially to save Elliott. I'll have to run it by General Fielding, though. There would be an awful lot of red tape to unscramble after this is all over, so he may veto the idea."

Travis rolled his eyes. The general could just get with the program. "Forget the red tape and make the call."

Tricia called her general and it was quickly apparent from her end of the conversation that Fielding didn't like the idea. He also didn't have a better alternative.

"It sounded as if he did more grumbling about red tape than you did," Travis noted as Tricia hung up. With any luck the old man felt as if he'd been handed a bomb to contain.

"It'll be his red tape to unscramble after all this is over. He left it to us to arrange everything. The paperwork on the base will have to be completely authentic. Elliott Harrison will be dead according to the military."

Travis pursed his lips. "Well, since you think someone on that base compromised Kelly, it's our only real option."

"Which puts the ball in your court," she said, grinning up at him. He couldn't resist kissing the smirk off her face. Tricia sighed when their lips parted. "I guess we'd better go talk to the Harrisons."

Now for the bad news. "We can't talk in the ICU waiting room. They mentioned that Taylor was by earlier checking on their son's condition. Taylor wasn't allowed in to see him but he managed to bug the waiting room."

"It's bugged?" she asked, looking a little paler.

He held up the neat little toy he'd picked up in D.C. a few months earlier. It looked like a cell phone. It wasn't. "Oh, yeah. I walked in there and this little puppy vibrated like there was no tomorrow. Luckily ICU was clean when we went in earlier. We'll take the Harrisons to their motel and talk to them on the way. I'll check their room when we get them there."

By the next morning in the ICU waiting room Harrison's parents began talking about the head injury and that their son had taken a turn for the worse because of it. Tricia made sure she was with them in the late afternoon when Dr. Adam Montgomery came in and told them the sad news that Elliott was gone. Adam was a surgeon but the excuse for his involvement was that he'd happened to go to ICU to check on a patient when the code blue was called. As the nearest doctor to the emergency he said he'd tried to help but there was nothing he could do.

Tricia reported that Adam, Elliott and the Harrisons all deserved Academy Awards for their performances. Travis had hated to ask Adam to essentially put his career on the line after all he'd been through because of Diablo and La Mano Oscura, but it had been his only option. Adam hadn't hesitated for a moment. He was eager to help put away the men tied to the doctor who'd tried to kill him and who'd held his now-wife captive.

Adam signed the death certificate at two and the pilot was "transferred" to the coroner, a friend of Sam. From there his body was "transferred" to a mortuary and cremated. The grieving parents left for Phoenix with their son's "remains" on Wednesday morning. Captain Elliott Harrison was transported not to the coroner's office but to a safe house arranged for by Adam's brother, Jake, thanks to his position with the FBI.

Wednesday night, clouds rolled in from the north, bringing frigid temperatures and the threat of an early snowfall. Travis decided to take his trusty four-wheel-drive Jeep on their little jaunt north for their planned incursion at Meadow Lake Airport. They left at seven, Tricia now ostensibly on leave. The skies grew more leaden as they drove out on I-24. It was fully dark by the time they arrived and snow began to fall just as they pulled off the road into a copse of trees across a field from the hangar housing the F-100 Super Sabre.

Their mission was to set up covert surveillance inside the hangar. And that was Travis's speciality. He'd gotten Jake to convince a federal judge that they had probable cause and she'd issued a warrant giving authorization for surveillance. Now all they had to do was get in and out with no one the wiser.

"You about ready?" he asked Tricia as he finished popping the lightbulb out of the interior light so it wouldn't flash on when they opened their doors to get out.

She huffed out a breath. "As I'll ever be. I wish the snow had held off. I don't like trailing footprints right up to the door."

"I hear you. But it can't be helped."

"So tell me again why *we're* doing this and not the FBI?" she asked with a wide grin. She knew very well why and answered her own question an instant later. "Oh, that's right. Because Travis doesn't like to share his toys."

"Travis's toys are better than theirs because Travis built them himself," he quipped right back, his mouth curving into a smile he just couldn't fight. Both of them had been doing a lot of smiling at each other since Sunday. They hadn't done much talking about their relationship or the past yet but none of that seemed to matter when they were looking into each other's eyes or working on the case.

He unlocked the gun safe behind his seat and handed her the 38mm semiautomatic, which she loaded and tucked into her midriff carry holster that nestled the weapon just below her bust line. He looked away to handle his own weapon, shoving a clip in the 38mm and sitting forward enough to slide it into the holster at the small of his back. Tricia tossed a black balaclava at him and pulled hers over her head, obscuring all but her eye and lip areas. He leaned forward and kissed her. "You have a very beautiful, very kissable mouth."

She laid her fingertip on his lips. "You must have kissed the Blarney Stone on one of those trips to Ireland I hear you've taken." She leaned forward and pulled his balaclava over his face. "The snow's picking up. Time for work." She opened her door and slid to the ground.

Travis got out, walked around to her side and handed her a pair of night vision goggles. He looked across the field. All looked quiet. He shouldered his backpack as Tricia pulled hers off the floor then donned it. She gave him a sharp nod once she'd tightened the belly strap.

"Let's do it then," he said, and they started across the field, bent low to minimize their silhouettes. Once at the hangar Tricia hunkered down to pick the key-in-knob lock like the pro he'd come to understand she was.

The toys Trish had teased him about were lipstick cameras with remote recording and access capabilities so there'd be no need for running wires or going back to collect tapes. And they could be switched off while the pilots swept the plane before take off. The real purpose was to record the contraband being taken off the F-100 after landing. And this way there'd be no reason for the kind of up-close-and-personal surveillance she'd been doing on her own. Even if the Bucs found the cameras, they'd have no idea who'd put them there.

The small access door soon fell open and he slipped inside as she stashed her picks and followed silently. The hangar was a steel building with an I-beam roof construction and had well-insulated walls and ceilings. The places where the insulation met the steel beams were the perfect hiding places for his little darlings.

Travis went right to work, carefully tossing a grappling hook up to the main ridge beam. It looped around and anchored perfectly. After a tug to make sure it was seated good and snug, he attached a motorized lifting motor to it and stepped into the loop that hung off the motor. Within thirty seconds he hooked his leg over the ridge beam and sent the motor down for Trish. As soon as she climbed onto the beam they separated and walked along the beam in opposite directions—she to the left and he to the right. Within half an hour the cameras were installed, well hidden and sending good strong signals to his ultra-thin, ultra-light laptop.

They sat on the beam as he checked all the cameras one more time with Tricia looking over his shoulder.

She grinned when he gave her a thumbs-up signal but then she froze and canted her head. And then he heard it, too. A car had pulled next to the building. Doors slammed shut. Travis pushed the screen on the laptop closed and stashed it back in his backpack before shouldering the pack again. Then he stretched out toward Trish, who'd worked hand over hand to pull the black nylon rope up to the rafters. "I locked the door again," she whispered as loud voices cut through the air.

He pointed to the corner of the area over the rest room and she nodded her understanding. If they could get there, they'd be relatively safe. But only if the falling snow had obliterated their prints. If not, they were probably going to have to shoot their way out of this.

The cubicle was behind him so he turned, and once he got his balance, walked the beam as quickly as he could to give Trish as much time as she needed. He hunkered down and lay flat, waiting for Trish to get to him.

Trish was still about fifteen feet out when her left foot slipped off the beam and she fell. Travis's heart stuttered as she caught herself practically in midair, leg looped over the beam, her arms dangling in the air. The lock rattled just as she pulled herself up onto the beam but time had run out. The door opened inward and a moment later a row of lights along the front of the hangar blasted on.

Tricia swung her legs behind her and lay flat along the beam, gripping it with her gloved hands and dropping her forehead to the cool steel beam. She looked like a bird on a wire out there. Ripe to be picked off from below. Travis started praying as he reached for his weapon. He'd never fired it at a human target before but he knew he'd kill to save her. With the clip loaded with magnum loads he knew he had the stopping power to do just that.

He was already asking forgiveness when he carefully took off the night vision goggles, quietly set them down on the roof of the rest room and took aim at the first one through the door. It was Taylor. Travis knew from instinct the pilot would kill her without a thought.

His heart pounded as he looked out at Tricia again. She lay there in the cloaking shadows of a long fluorescent light fixture that hung a few feet below her. She was safe as long as she didn't attract attention. Then he noticed her backpack slipping.

He checked his target again then glanced back at her. She'd bent her left arm, holding the beam at about her waist, her crooked elbow keeping the pack from falling. Travis blinked as perspiration ran into his eyes. It was freezing in the hangar but he knew it was the situation that had him sweating. He slowly wiped his eyes across his sleeve, continuing to hold a firing position.

Travis looked back down at the two men who'd entered last. Mitch Simpson and Reggie Edwards walked to the workbench on the back wall and stood directly under Tricia. "So you figure we're off the hook for Harrison?" Simpson asked Edwards as he rooted around for something.

"I told you all along we were careful," Taylor said,

joining them at the bench. "Unlike you, who left the key to the safe deposit box out here."

"Yeah, yeah," Simpson replied. "So we had to drive a few miles. Big deal. I'm more worried about Streeter trying to investigate what really happened to Harrison. You said he struggled. What if the coroner saw bruises?"

"They cremated him. They don't do that if they're suspicious. Quit borrowing trouble. The coroner probably blamed any bruises on the nurses or the ambulance transport team. The note convinced the general it was suicide. Streeter's boyfriend seemed convinced. And you think Streeter would have taken leave if she thought her bud had been murdered? Look at the way she got herself assigned to Kelly's case. We're in the clear."

"I still think Rule and Walters liked helping kill Kelly a little too much," Simpson complained.

"Hey, the guy kept them out of top gun. He had it coming," Taylor said, then chuckled. "And they sure liked making Harrison beg then holding him down while I shot him up."

"He has a point. What if you can't control them?" Edwards asked.

"Look, they're handy to have around. If Streeter gets close to us on the Kelly murder, we can give her to them."

"Streeter's looking real good these days," Edwards said.

"Hey," Simpson protested, "if we're passing out assignments, I'd just as soon see you pass her my way," Simpson said. "I'm the one with a score to settle with her."

Travis's finger just itched to squeeze off a round.

Lord, help me, he prayed. *I don't think I've ever needed Your grace more.*

Edwards laughed. "You'd need a little help with her. You owe her but she did clean your clock last month in that martial-arts demo General Fielding cooked up." He walked over to a window and looked out. "Hey, you two, the snow's really piling up out there. Find the blasted key and let's get back to base."

Simpson cursed and said he'd found the key they'd been looking for, then they all moved toward the door. Neither Travis not Trish moved until the car pulled away.

Only then did he move. He holstered his weapon, put on the goggles, then walked the beam toward her. "You okay?" he asked.

She pushed herself up slowly. "I'll live," she said, her voice tight. "Were the cameras recording? Please tell me we got all that on tape."

"We got it. Now let's get us down from here. I don't know about you, but I need a hug."

Chapter Fifteen

Tricia hooked her right foot in the loop and flipped the switch to let herself to the floor. Her left leg and hip were in screaming agony, but when Travis grabbed her by the shoulders and pulled her into his arms, she forgot everything. He was so big. So solid. And he'd been worried—about her. No one had ever worried about her except Travis. It used to make her feel weak and ineffectual. Now it just felt…right.

He squeezed her one last time then said, "Okay. Now I think I can say this." He stepped away, keeping his hands on her shoulders. "Don't ever scare me like that again. My heart couldn't take it."

She shivered in the chill air, all of a sudden aware that her hair under the balaclava was soaking wet. She glanced up at the structure above then back at him. Like her, he still wore the concealing ski mask and night vision goggles. "I'm so sorry. I could have given us away. I can't believe I was so clumsy."

"Clumsy? The way you caught yourself then managed to swing back up onto the beam looked more like a controlled gymnastic move than clumsiness," he said before turning to unhook the motor and press a button on the end of the nylon cord that apparently unhooked the grappling arms and let them go slack. Travis yanked and the cord fell into his hands.

"Hey, cool gizmo," she said, but grimaced, thinking that her movement up there when she'd managed to catch herself had been more desperation than any demonstration of grace. She didn't know if her leg would hold her weight. "Guess it's time we blew this pop stand," she quipped, and took a step. Sucking a high-pitched breath when pain exploded down her leg from hip to knee, Tricia crumpled. The room exploded in what looked like fireworks—but they were on the inside of her eyelids.

"Whoa," Travis said. He wrapped his arm around her waist and braced her upright with his hip. "You're hurt!"

She took a deep shaky breath and nodded. "Guess so. My hip, I think."

"Uh-oh. Catching yourself like that probably dislocated it. I'd better carry you before you make it worse." Even though he'd announced his intention, she yelped when he scooped her up in his arms and started for the door.

"You can't carry me all the way to the car in a snowstorm. You'll hurt your back."

He chuckled. "Yeah, right. You don't weigh that much."

"Last week you said I was fat," she told him as he stopped at the door.

"I did not. Besides, I was a lot dumber last week. You have to overlook anything I said then. Now unlock the door like a good little secret agent and we'll be on our way."

The trip to the Jeep wasn't particularly easy on either of them but Travis barely faltered. Before she knew it, he set her on the seat and pulled off his goggles and ski mask. She did the same and his hand was immediately in her hair. "You're soaked to the skin. I don't know if I should take you to the E.R. or home to change first."

"Home. We can't go to the E.R. like this. We look like we've been out for a night of B and E."

Travis snorted irreverently but his smile was gentle. "We were, sweetheart," he said, and closed her door, leaving her in stunned silence. Sweetheart? He called her sweetheart.

Wow!

Travis climbed in next to her and didn't seem to notice that the world had shifted. That life as she'd known it had exploded into something so beautiful and exciting, she felt as if she were standing in the center of a meteor shower.

He went about the business of locking up their weapons and started the engine. Before putting it in gear, though, he looked over at her, his expression thoughtful. Eyes narrowed as if still thinking even as he spoke, he said, "You know what? It's fun working together, huh?"

He didn't wait for an answer, which was a good thing since she'd already been speechless. He just beamed at her and backed the Jeep out of the cover of the little copse of trees. Travis had come so far.

They'd come so far.

Then her heart did a little bottomless dip. Would he still feel this way about her if she proved one of the men behind the syndicate was Max Vance?

She'd lain up there on that beam, suspended above the three pilots, praying they wouldn't spot her. Praying for Travis's safety if they did. But most of all, praying for an end to the uncertainty. If only they'd just gone ahead and said the names of their boss and his cohort in crime.

The Jeep fishtailed when the front tires hit the asphalt of the road next to the airport, and worry and anxiety fled in a shower of real physical agony.

"Are you all right?" Travis asked when he got control of the vehicle.

She gritted her teeth and nodded but it was a big fat lie.

Travis didn't seem to notice but tuned into an all-news radio station and they learned they were in the middle of a full-scale blizzard. The weather report had changed. Forecasters were now calling for thirty-nine inches before morning. Two hours had come and gone after that first slide when she saw the Vance Memorial Hospital sign glowing through the nearly horizontal snow.

"When did we change destinations?"

Travis pulled the Jeep under an overhang and turned in his seat. Trish looked beat. "When I saw how much that bumpy start hurt you." He got out and came around to her door. "Ready?" he asked when he pulled it open.

She had her head back against the headrest and her eyes closed. "Ready as I'll ever be. I just hope they don't arrest us on suspicion of burglary." Her smile was brave but unconvincing as he cradled her in his arms and carried her inside. The last thing he expected to see as the doors swished closed behind him was his mother's nephew, his hand wrapped in a towel.

"Alessandro?" he asked. "I didn't know you were in town."

"Travis!" his cousin said in slightly accented English as he jumped to his feet. "You have found a damsel in distress. Ah, and a very pretty one, too."

"Major Patricia Streeter. Trish, this is Alessandro Donato, a cousin on my mother's side of the family," Travis explained even as he wondered what it was about Alessandro that troubled him. Then he noticed Tricia staring not at Alessandro's handsome face but at the way he was dressed—exactly the way he and Trish were. He'd told Trish there was nothing suspicious about dressing in all black but if that was true, then why did it look sinister on Alessandro?

Travis set Tricia in a chair and her hiss of pain went through him like a knife. He squatted down next to her, noting how pale she'd grown. Once again he asked himself how he could have so strong a connection to her so soon. Maybe because it wasn't soon at all, but more on the order of *still*. Did that mean he still loved her, too? That was where he'd been headed since that kiss in the alley so maybe it was time to face the truth.

"How did you hurt yourself, *bella signorina?*" Alessandro asked, the unfamiliar cadence of his accent pulling Travis out of his thoughts.

Travis gritted his teeth. The guy was just too smooth. He charmed women easily but so did Jake Montgomery and that didn't set his teeth on edge the way Alessandro's charm did. He didn't seem to do it in the unconscious, natural-born way Jake did. The European charm came across as too studied, too deliberate. Look at the way he was bending over backward to charm Trish…while he was bleeding into a towel! And Trish was pale, in considerable pain and looked like a drowned rat. A pretty rat but his cousin hadn't called her *bel topo,* had he?

"We went sledding. I slipped and fell," Tricia lied smoothly in answer to his cousin's question about her mishap. "How did you cut your hand?" she went on to ask, obviously not charmed at all.

Her lack of response to him brought Alessandro up short. He stared for a long moment then blinked. "Glass. I broke a glass. Foolish. I feel very foolish."

Travis grinned. "Better watch it, cuz. Trish doesn't suffer fools too well."

Tricia, Travis noticed, had been spending her time watching his reaction to his Italian cousin, which meant he'd given away his feelings. He forced a chuckle and a grin. "At least that was what she told me not long ago when I was the fool. I'm going to sign you in before someone else gets ahead of you, sweetheart. You sit tight."

He'd taken one step when he realized they had a problem. If she lied to the E.R. doctors about how she'd fallen, they might become suspicious of the injury or worse, misdiagnose her injury.

Then like a gift from above, as he walked toward the sign-in window, he heard Adam Montgomery call his name from a doorway across the hall. "Adam! Just the man I need."

"Which is getting to be a habit."

"Same station, new problem. I brought Trish in. I think she may have dislocated her hip. At least I'm hoping that's all she did. The thing is, she got hurt when she nearly fell from a roof beam. She was helping me plant surveillance equipment out at Meadow Lake Airport. I don't want to have to lie to the E.R. guys about how she did it. I'm afraid it might throw off a diagnosis or raise eyebrows about the obvious lie. Her thigh is probably already Technicolor."

"Why don't I take a look at her up in my office? I'm not an orthopedist but you aren't going to get one to-night anyway."

Travis looked back and saw a nurse leading Alessandro through the E.R. doors. "Great. I'll bring her right up."

Four hours and one horrible ride home later Tricia closed her eyes as he settled an ice bag on her hip. "Oh, that feels so good. So tell me why you don't like your cousin Alessandro."

"I just can't trust him. I don't think he's being up-front about what he does for a living, for one thing. I don't know what he is but I don't think he's doing ac-counting for the European Union."

"Hmm. Maybe he's an international jewel thief. He was certainly dressed like one." She grinned. "Oh, but then, so were we," she teased.

Which only reminded him of how she'd gotten hurt. He couldn't forget seeing her slip, fall, catch herself, then hang suspended above the jet. The memory had his pulse skittering all over again. Those had been the longest ten seconds of his life to date. If she hadn't caught herself… He ran a nervous hand through his hair then noticed Tricia watching him. "I can't leave you this way," he told her.

"I'd be fine." She glanced out the window. "But I'm just not sure you *can* leave. Or at least that it would be smart to go back out in this."

"But if I stay, it'll be all over the base by morning that I stayed here. It doesn't look right. I don't care for me but…"

She smiled. "I'll be on crutches for at least three days. Adam said maybe even a week. I don't think the talk will be all that licentious if anyone even notices your Jeep in the drive buried under thirty some inches of snow. They'll assume you were taking care of me."

She had a point—he guessed. "I guess so. I'll carry you into your room and take the sofa."

"Oh, no, you won't," she said with an emphatic shake of her head. "I'm not moving again till morning. These scrubs Adam lent me are comfortable and dry and you won't fit on this sofa. I hate books and movies that have a five-foot-two-inch heroine taking the bed when the six-foot-two-inch hero has to sleep on a sofa that's too short for him."

"You're five-nine," he argued.

"I'm still fine right here. I'm comfortable. I sleep here by accident all the time. Now go to bed."

He wasn't convinced.

"Shoo!"

Travis shrugged. When she got like this it was time to throw in the towel, he thought. He must be learning. "Okay, okay. I'm going. Promise to call if you need anything."

"Scout's honor."

He got halfway to the bedroom door and turned, his eyes narrowed. "You were never a scout," he accused.

She laughed. "No, but I'm honorable. Now go to bed!"

He went.

Chapter Sixteen

As Adam had predicted, Tricia was well past the use of crutches by Sunday morning. The weather was sunny and warm again in typical Colorado style. There was little evidence of the snow that had stopped the city in its tracks Wednesday night. The melt had begun with sunny and warm sixty-degree weather the day after the blizzard and had continued in the same vein. Being from Pennsylvania she didn't think she'd ever get used to blizzards in October or snow that disappeared almost overnight.

After explaining to Lidia and Max that they had other plans for the day, she and Travis left the church, foregoing the social after the service and dinner with his parents. Tricia gave up trying to keep up with Travis halfway down the steps. He stormed ahead, his shoulders hunched, his hands shoved in his pockets. Then he stopped short as if he'd run into a brick wall and turned back, a dark frown in place as he waited for her to catch up.

"Sorry," he muttered, holding out his hand to her.

She considered not taking it for about half a second but relented. She'd hoped going to church would keep him marching along the path to healing, not bring him down. "Want to tell me what has you so upset?"

"Not upset. Not really mad." He shrugged. "Annoyed, I guess. Maybe. I don't know. It just bugs me."

"Church bugged you?"

He shook his head. "No. I like Gabriel Dawson's style, and what Sam did with the choir today was great."

"Okay. So did your parents say something I missed before we left? Are they upset that we skipped out on dinner?"

He shook his head and let go of her hand to unlock the door of the Jeep. "It's that business with Emily."

Ah. His brother Peter's ex-wife. "You're annoyed because we prayed for Emily Armstrong's safety?"

"Not the prayer. No. I just can't believe she'd signed up to go to Venezuela to help reopen the Doctors Without Borders clinic. Especially after Adam was nearly killed in that very clinic," Travis groused as she climbed into the Jeep.

Where was the mystery? Tricia wondered as he circled the hood. "I don't know her very well but she's a good doctor," Tricia told him. "And she wants to help people. I'm sure she must think she's needed more down there than she is here."

"She was never particularly adventurous when she was with Peter," he groused. "Just the opposite, in fact. After Peter was nearly killed in an explosion, he needed her but that didn't seem to matter to her. She still left him. Living a safe, predictable life was all she cared about. It reminded me of the way Allison acted about the police force."

"You sound as if you blame Emily for the divorce *and* Peter's disappearance, but your parents were the ones who asked Pastor Gabriel to pray for her safety. They don't blame her, but you do?" she asked, wanting to understand how his mind worked.

To his credit, he thought for a moment. "That would be sort of a yes and no answer. I don't think Peter wanted the divorce, and I know a broken heart when I see one, no matter what my brother said. But, as for him being gone all this time, Peter got on that plane of his own free will. He headed to wherever he is and he hasn't seen fit to come back or contact us. That's all on him."

"So you don't think he's dead?"

He shook his head, and put the vehicle in gear. "No. Not at all. He's out there somewhere doing—" he hesitated "—whatever it is he does. I worry about him one day and the next I want to get my hands on him for worrying Mom like this. When I see him again, I'll probably hug him then punch his lights out."

She had to laugh at the typical Travis reaction. In the past several days she'd seen him irritable and gentle by turns. His irritability over the things the Buccaneers had said about hurting her and his gentleness over her and her injury came to mind.

"Do you think your parents believed our excuse about today?"

Ever changeable, he grinned. "Not for a minute. They

think I just want you all to myself." He looped an arm over her shoulders and chuckled as he kissed her. "And they'd be right."

But once they entered the house, they weren't entirely alone. The Buccaneers, Diablo and La Mano Oscura seemed to step inside with them. Because looming on the wall was the map of the lower half of North, Central and the upper half of South America.

"Well, I guess it's time to get back to this." She walked to the map and just stared. Travis followed and stood at her side surveying all they'd accomplished the day before.

Five sets of colored pins marked the flight towers each of the Bucs had checked in with. The pins were linked with thread. The threads were cut to the scale of the map and represented the total miles Captain Johnston had logged for each of the mystery flights. And hanging off the last known check-in point for each flight going out and coming back was a loop of thread that represented the unaccounted-for miles.

At three, Tricia finished up the calculation on that last flight Bruce Taylor flew—the one where she'd been tailing him but had run into Travis. "That's it," she said. "Now we see if Ian's La Mano Oscura/Diablo theory holds water."

Travis started stretching out the loop of unaccounted-for miles. "Brazil, Peru." He tossed his hands up in disgust after the third flight netted the same result.

"I can't believe Ian was wrong."

"Well, this isn't proving a thing," he said, crossing

his arms. "Why? I really thought we had it. I was so sure he and Sam called it right."

She still thought they had it. "This makes no sense. La Mano Oscura and Diablo have to be linked. There's just too much of a coincidence floating around. Adam Montgomery was shot in the robbery of a Venezuelan clinic in La Mano Oscura territory. Dr. Valenti came back here and tried to kill him to protect his identity. Then Valenti gets killed by Jaramillo, a Venezuelan in jail here, in Diablo territory."

Travis was nodding. "I agree," he said, a frown crinkling his brow as he stood deep in thought. Travis tapped the map. "But the miles don't lie. We have too many miles for the Bucs to be stopping in Venezuela."

Travis checked his watch, his expression and tone full of disgust. "And now we have to go meet Herr General Fielding." His German accent was bad but it got his opinion of the military across loud and clear. How was she going to keep Travis in her life and keep her career when he had such a bad attitude toward the very foundation of her life? She'd seen a number of marriages fall apart when the spouse was only indifferent toward the military. Travis seemed to outright hate it.

Feeling defensive, Tricia said, "You don't have to come."

He raised an eyebrow. "Am I not spit and polish enough to meet your boss?"

"I thought maybe he'd be too spit and polish for you." She shrugged. "Maybe I am, too."

* * *

Travis could happily have cut out his tongue. He'd lived for nearly four years listening to Allison making snide remarks about everything from his uniform to the ties his boss wore to the precinct Christmas party. He would *not* do this to Trish, no matter how much he resented the Air Force and their autocratic attitude. But for the first time he understood how Allison had felt. He'd been a cop at heart and Tricia seemed to feel the same way toward the Air Force. She'd risen to the rank of major and on base she was given all the respect and deference that classification afforded her. He was proud of her accomplishments; he just wasn't sure he could live with the military bossing around his woman.

Whoa. His mother, not to mention Tricia, would box his ears if he ever actually came out and said what he'd been thinking. But he was very much coming to think of Trish as his. So what was he going to do with his lousy attitude?

If he loved her—and he was more than a little sure he did— only one answer came to mind: adjust it.

The general beat them to the restaurant. Travis braced for a snide remark but Fielding only smiled and stood while Tricia sat after an obligatory salute. He got though that without a smart remark and was feeling hopeful that he could hold his tongue. Until the general asked Tricia—actually, he ordered her—to go powder her nose.

"Excuse me?" she asked, looking as nonplussed as Travis had ever seen her.

"I said go powder you nose or whatever it is you women do in bathrooms that takes so long. Go, Major. Now."

Tricia stood and left. He noticed she didn't think to take her purse, and she looked nervous and upset. He didn't blame her.

"Now we can talk," Fielding said.

Travis ignored him, watching Trish until she entered the ladies' lounge. "Yeah, we can talk." He pointed at the older man. "I'll talk and you listen, chrome dome. She's military. I'm not. I ever hear you talk to her that way and you'll be looking up at me from the floor. Got it?"

Rather than get equally angry, Fielding threw back his shaved head and laughed. "That's the best laugh I've had in weeks," he admitted, wiping tears from his eyes. "Tell me, does Major Streeter know you're in love with her?"

Since he himself had only just figured that part out, Travis pretty much doubted she did. And didn't intend to tell her until he knew what he was prepared to do about it. "My feelings for Trish are irrelevant," he told Fielding.

"Not to me they aren't," Fielding said, then took a sip of his soda. "You stayed with her the night of the storm and I know that isn't her usual style. It's one of the many things I admire about her."

So much for no one noticing or caring about his Jeep. "She was hurt, as she reported to you. I stayed to make sure she was okay. That's all there was to it."

The general looked unimpressed. "I don't care what did or didn't happen that night. I just don't want to see you hurt her again. From something she said, I gathered you did once. I don't have a daughter but if I did—"

Travis gritted his teeth. "If you *were* her father, I'd lay you out flat right here for the childhood she had.

Maybe *that's* where you ought to be looking for past hurts," Travis said, but that didn't stop him from feeling guilty. He *had* hurt Tricia. But he wasn't about to do it again, so he guessed he appreciated her commanding officer caring this much about her.

Fielding stared at him then nodded in that sharp military way Tricia did. "That's good to know. I'm glad you're there to watch her back. Now tell me what you've collected on this crew." He leaned forward and his gaze sharpened. "And their bosses."

"We have tape from the hangar. Taylor implicated Rule and Walters in Kelly's murder and they're the ones who held Harrison down when Taylor shot him up with the drugs."

Tricia was suddenly at his side. And she was *not* happy. "May I ask a question off the record, sir?" she asked the general. When he nodded, she demanded, "Can the little woman join the Neanderthals or am I still banished to the little girl's room?"

It was Travis's turn to laugh. At least until Tricia turned her furious gaze on him. He held his hands up, palms outward, in a sign of surrender. "Hey, just cheering you on, sweetheart. The private conference wasn't my idea, remember." And not for a million bucks would he repeat what that conference had been about. He wasn't suicidal. She'd take a strip off both of them if she knew, and on a more serious note, though he wasn't crazy about the military, he wouldn't do anything to hurt her career.

"So...*Major.*" General Fielding paused as if to remind her that they were back on the record. Her attention shifted as did her posture in some nearly imperceptible way that said the general had his major back. Then he continued. "I just asked your partner about the surveillance and he tells me there isn't any doubt we'll be able to nail Ian's murderers."

"Two of them. Apparently it took three. We still don't know who they assisted, sir." Tricia admitted. "It could be General Hadley or it could be Diablo's ringleader."

Fielding cleared his throat. "No matter how high-placed Hadley's partner is, no matter *who* he is, I expect you two to bring him down, as well. I want the head cut off this particular snake in paradise. How about Johnston's information? Did that lead to any discoveries?"

She didn't sigh in disgust but it was there in her eyes. "We thought we'd be able to link La Mano Oscura and Diablo but intelligence says the cartel operates out of Venezuela. Our mileage figures show the Bucs may be flying as far as Peru or Brazil."

"Are you sure?" he asked, a frown wrinkling his forehead. "That makes no sense."

Tricia shrugged. "Unless they do a lot of airport hopping after their last tower check-in."

"What about refueling?" Fielding asked.

Travis snapped his fingers and looked at Tricia. "That's what was wrong with the figures. They don't land in the U.S., but to get to Venezuela they have to stop to refuel."

Tricia's eyes brightened. "And I'll bet they all stop off at the same airstrip—La Mano Oscura's airstrip—so it's no questions asked. The Super Sabre is too distinctive not to raise questions about frequent stop-offs."

Travis glanced at his watch. "We have a pilot landing up at Meadow Lake and we need to tail him. This could be the break we need," he said and stood to leave. After what happened on their last trip up there, he hated that Tricia insisted on going along but this was her investigation. He wondered how he was going to get used to her placing herself in danger.

Driving as fast as he dared, Travis made it to Meadow Lake before Walters landed the Sabre. He parked in the same copse of trees and waited. And waited. And waited some more. Walters didn't land. At midnight they started splitting the watch. Tricia's phone rang at dawn. It was General Fielding.

Walters had called in from Dallas with engine trouble. He was flying in commercially and had called to extend his weekend leave by a day. The Sabre was grounded until repairs were complete, stalling the major part of the investigation for the near future.

They each went home for a little sleep, then met back at Travis's place to start on the map that afternoon. Pretty soon they found that the Yucatán Peninsula in southern Mexico had to be the place La Mano Oscura had an airstrip. After that, the mileage figures narrowed to flights to Ecuador, Colombia, Venezuela or the southern Antilles. They were banking on Venezuela and La Mano Oscura.

But how to prove the link while the plane was grounded?

Chapter Seventeen

"Just what we needed," Travis muttered from behind the lens of Tricia's camera. "Another suspect or something else suspicious happening in town."

Tricia stopped posing by the tree and walked back toward him. They'd gone to the park as a break from searching satellite images of the Yucatán for a landing strip big enough to set down an F-100.

Travis pointed to the bottom of the hill and handed her the camera, the lens in zoom position. "Don't this beat all. It looks like the walk in the park isn't going to be a walk in the park after all. 'No rest for the weary,' my mother always says."

She took the camera, adjusted the focus slightly and there, in the center of the park, stood Travis's cousin Alessandro, talking to a flamboyantly dressed man in his mid-fifties. The older man looked vaguely familiar but she couldn't place him. He had reddish hair styled in the worst comb-over she'd ever seen. There was a woman on his arm Tricia might have mistaken for a streetwalker were it not for the expensive fox jacket she wore.

Tricia had to admit this was the last sort of man she would have expected to see with the suave Alessandro Donato. "Which one do you suspect of something? The middle-aged comb-over, the call girl or the playboy? And what for? Fashion faux pas of the rich and sleazy?"

"Smart mouth. We're looking for someone highly placed in society. That's Alistair Barclay talking to my cousin of the questionable scruples and even more questionable profession. The woman is just Barclay's usual window dressing."

Barclay. She'd seen him announcing his candidacy on television. He looked thinner but smarmier in person. And she hadn't trusted Travis's cousin from the second he'd opened his mouth. But she'd been thinking of the number of broken hearts he'd left behind him and not lives shattered by drugs.

"Ah. The bad vibes I picked up on between you and cousin Alessandro in the E.R. What do you mean 'questionable profession'?"

"Does *that* look like an accountant to you?"

"No, but then Barclay doesn't look like a mayoral candidate or a hotel tycoon, either. He looks like a pawnshop owner or a P.I. Oops, sorry. Didn't mean to disparage your chosen profession."

"I'm a security expert, not a P.I. Huge difference," he said.

She glanced at Travis, then back through her viewfinder to take a few shots. They were a trio of questionable characters to be sure, but this could easily be an innocent meeting between an international businessman and an accountant for the European Union where Barclay probably had hotels.

"Are you sure you aren't overreacting? They might have a legitimate reason to meet. Some of Barclay's hotels are in Europe. Has your cousin done anything suspicious other than flirt with me, have a suave accent and dress too well to be an accountant?"

"Sam doesn't like him, either. And this is their second meeting. They were together at the bachelor auction."

Travis's participation in the Galilee Women's Shelter's big fund-raiser in September had kept her from attending. But the Lord clearly had had plans for her that hiding at home that night had not thwarted. She'd met up with Travis anyway, thank the Lord.

"Did you really take some poor woman to a ball game and dinner at the ballpark?" she teased.

He scowled and said, "Hey. We went in a limo, those were box seats and it was a gourmet meal. She knew what she bought."

Thinking of Travis's attitude when they first met again, Tricia chuckled. "Yeah, dinner with Oscar the Grouch and the Broncos. And I hear you watched a baseball game on the limo's TV on the way."

"It was a play-off game," he defended himself. "How do you know that, anyway?"

"I was at the shelter when your date called Jessica to complain."

"And what did my sister-in-law say?"

Tricia checked the progress of the meeting below. "That the dates were for charity and hadn't come with a guarantee of a good time, a proposal or a refund."

His glare grew more intense. "Get serious or give me back the camera so I can watch."

She fought the twitch of her lips trying to smile. "They just shook hands and turned and walked away from each other. Alessandro is climbing into a rental and Barclay is headed farther across the lawns to his limo. Do you want to try following one of them?"

"Nah. We'd never get to that lot in time. Besides, you're probably right. They may have a legitimate reason to meet. I just hope there wasn't an *illegitimate* one. My mother's crazy about Alessandro."

"Maybe she sees something in him we don't."

"It wouldn't be the first time."

Max Vance popped into Tricia's thoughts. *Or the first time she was wrong?*

"Speaking of Mom, let's stop in at the café. Wednesday's special is her lobster-and-portobello ravioli."

Now that piqued her interest. Travis might not have been cooking for himself over the years but he knew where to go for the best food in town.

When they arrived, Sam was hugging his mother. The lunch specials were posted and sure enough Travis knew exactly what was on the menu for that day. "Hey. It's the big-time P.I., Mom," Sam called out.

"I am not a P.I. P.I.'s spy on people and take pictures."

Tricia snorted, their last activity popping into her head. Travis shot a glare her way.

Sam laughed and clapped Travis on the back. "I'm missing my B-Ball partner. What's keeping you so busy? Maybe we can share a table and catch up."

Travis looked around. "Subtle, bro. Translation— Sam wants an update," he told her under his breath. "Suppose we do takeout. Do you have time to come up to my place?"

Sam arched a questioning brow. "Is this official?"

"As official as it gets in this thing," Travis said, shrugging. "That's okay, isn't it, sweetheart?"

She nodded, speechless, nearly breathless. He'd called her sweetheart again. And in front of his mother. *And* his brother. Maybe she had reason to hope he planned to stay in her life after the case was solved. But how long could *she* stay in *his* life? How long before orders were cut that would send her away from Colorado Springs? From him?

Lidia and Fiona fussed over the triple order, then Tricia followed Travis and Sam who'd gone ahead to get in a fast game of one-on-one, or as most sane people would call it, cutthroat basketball.

Both men were sweating profusely when she arrived at Travis's house. Sam had on the most disreputable sweat suit she'd ever seen. But when she looked at it further, she realized it had been Travis's University of Pennsylvania warm-up suit.

"Couldn't you find something better to loan your brother?"

"He tells me this is a collector's item," Sam said, wearing a goofy grin. The two brothers lost ten years apiece on the maturity scale the second they stepped on to a basketball court.

"Uh-huh, sure," she mocked.

Cody ran around the building chasing a rabbit. "Sit!" Travis shouted. Cody immediately broke off the chase and did as ordered. "Stay," he added, then rewarded the big dog with an affectionate ruff scratching.

She blinked, staring at the usually effusive dog. "I didn't know he was that well trained," she said.

"He's never shown you what Cody can do? Travis Maxwell Vance, for shame," Sam scolded. "Hiding Cody's light under a bushel. Tsk. Tsk."

Travis walked toward the two of them, dribbling the basketball as if it were still an involuntary response like breathing. "Can it, Sam. He doesn't listen around Trish. He tends to get distracted around her."

Remembering the way the shepherd disobeyed Travis the day she'd first come to the house, she understood. She looked back at the dog and had to chuckle. Sure enough Cody had begun creeping toward her. "Uh, Trav…Cody's not staying put."

Travis turned, dropping the ball, and planted his hands on his hips. Cody stopped dead, rolled on his side and looked around trying to look innocent. Sam burst out laughing.

"Cody, get Sam. Get him," Travis ordered, and Cody hit the ground running, bowling Sam over. They wrestled for a few seconds, Cody growling and sounding ferocious. The Sam yelled that he'd given up and Cody stood still with his front paws on Sam's chest.

"Guard," Travis told him. Cody sat next to Sam then leaned forward and growled in Sam's face when he shifted a little.

"Release," Travis ordered, and Cody bounded back to him.

Next the men grabbed padding and worked the dog, taking turns being handler and attacker. It was an impressive demonstration. "How come you have him trained?" Tricia asked.

Travis tossed Sam a towel and looped one around his own neck after wiping his face. "I take him with me on cases where I need backup. He's also a good tracker."

"Smart dog, aren't you, boy?" Sam rubbed Cody's ruff and got his face washed by Cody's grateful tongue. Sam checked his watch. "Okay, you two, I have to get going. I'll have to run home and shower before heading back to the station. How about you tell me what's up over lunch?" Sam suggested.

Travis scooped up the meals and they all trooped into the kitchen. He sat on his kitchen counter and she and Sam took the bar stools at the breakfast bar.

Sam turned around and glanced around at Travis's "office." "Man, would you *do* something with this place? If not for yourself then the rest of us."

"So…how are things at the department?" Travis asked, ignoring Sam's remarks about the house as he dug into the meal his mother had sent.

Sam shot Tricia a look that said the ball was in her court as far as the house went, then admitted, "The *department's* sinking under the pressure of this crime wave. If we don't do something soon, we're all going to be calling Alistair Barclay 'Mr. Mayor.' Even if Frank Montgomery doesn't run, anybody his party picks won't win if this continues. This morning Barclay held a press conference and blamed the administration and CSPD for all the problems. A poll the *Sentinel* ran said the majority of citizens are swallowing his rhetoric—hook, line and sinker. It's a pretty simplistic analysis of a complex problem, but in a sad way it makes sense. If we'd been able to crack the drug ring, maybe this crime wave wouldn't have happened, and Barclay wouldn't be ahead in the polls."

Travis grimaced. "Now I really wish we had better news for you, bro. The truth is, we could cut the supply line today with the evidence we have already. We could have done it last week."

Sam's eyes glittered with anticipation. "Tell me you've got a good reason to wait."

"Remember the note the CSI's found stuffed in the bottom of Kelly's pocket?"

Sam nodded. "It's the reason I asked you to follow up. My DEA contact says they're trying to get people in place but, as I said, we're swamped *now.*"

"It looks as if you and Kelly were right," Travis told him, and then explained about what had happened and what they'd heard in the hangar. "The stuff is probably coming in from the area of Venezuela that's La Mano Oscura's territory. We don't have the exact location nailed down yet."

Sam's shoulders sagged as he took a bite of ravioli.

"I'd hoped against hope I was wrong. That it was idle speculation."

"So, do you understand?" she asked. "If I arrest the pilots, another route will just open up. We've got to sit on what we know and use it to get to the top. We're pretty sure we know who organized the pilots. It's his community contact—the head of Diablo—that we haven't nailed down. And if we can hang in there long enough, we might be able to get the Venezuela connection, as well. Think how much good that would do worldwide."

"Well, I may have found another link. We arrested Ernesto Ramirez, the guy you saw with the pilot in that alley in the beginning of the month. Immigration tells us he came here from Venezuela to join his cousin Jorge Jaramillo—Valenti's killer. So I guess we sit tight and wait." Sam ran a hand through his hair and grinned. "There have to be worse things than calling Barclay 'Mr. Mayor' for the next four years."

"By the way, on the subject of Barclay…" Travis said. "We saw cousin Alessandro with him again."

"Barclay has hotels in the European Union." Sam shrugged. "I guess they could have dealings with each other."

"You're going soft with all this love-and-marriage stuff. You didn't like Barclay at first. And I still say Alessandro's no accountant," Travis grumbled.

Sam arched one eyebrow. "What does an accountant look like? I mean, does Jake look like a computer geek? Do you?"

Tricia laughed at Travis's glare.

He crossed his arms and leaned back against the upper cabinets. "I still think we should have warned Mom not to give Alessandro any of her nest egg to invest."

Sam grinned and said, "*I'm* not telling her. Risk your own head. Me, I'm off to shower, change and get back to work. Take it easy, you two. Go careful out there."

Tricia turned away. *Go careful out there.* That was what Max had said on the phone. Another familiar saying among the Vance men. His sons were going to be devastated and all she could do was try protecting their reputations by keeping them in the dark.

Please, Lord. When the time comes to tell him, let him understand.

Chapter Eighteen

Travis watched Tricia pace to the map on the wall, shake her head then stalk back and flop on the sectional sofa he'd rented for the living room the week before. The dining room was still set up as a home office but now the living room looked comfortable and inviting.

"Antsy?" he asked, grinning at her. She ignored him and glared at the computer screen as if it had become her mortal enemy. He'd set his laptop on the coffee table with the surveillance program running so they could watch the Meadow Lake hangar at their leisure. They'd been watching it almost around the clock ever since losing Edwards in traffic Sunday night.

"How about this?" she said. "We get a warrant and go see what's in that safe-deposit box."

Travis shook his head and put his feet up on a pillow on the coffee table. He reached along the back of the sofa and fingered her hair, hoping to help her unwind a little. "It's not worth the risk, sweetheart," he told her. "They may only have money in there. It'd be evidence for a trial but it isn't going to get us anywhere nearer to the top and we both know it. Will you try to relax?"

"*You* relax. It's been a week and that computer screen hasn't changed! Can't they at least get together and wash the jet? Maybe they'd slip and say something incriminating. The general's really on my case. He wants results. All I had to report in my weekly briefing was more evidence against the Bucs and an accident that kept us from following the package after Sunday's drop."

"It couldn't be helped. A tractor-trailer jackknifed in front of us. If we were dead, would he like that excuse better? I still don't know how you avoided sliding us under it. "

"Tell that to General Fielding." She stopped and stared at him as if remembering their encounter at the restaurant. "No. On second thought, don't ever talk to him again. He's been acting strangely ever since. What *did* you two talk about while I was banished to the ladies' room? You've never said."

The more he thought about that conversation, the more it bugged Travis. Not the stuff about Trish and how he felt about her. Annoying as it had been he was glad, in a way, her boss cared enough about her to ask the tough question. It was the wrap-up of that talk and Fielding's attitude toward them exposing Diablo's leader. Why wouldn't they bring the guy down? He deserved to live out his years behind bars. One thing was for sure, Trish deserved to know about the general's attitude.

"You know I'm not quite sure what Fielding was after. He acted as if we might pull our punches because

of what Taylor said about Diablo being run by a leading citizen with a lot to lose. What do either of us care
what people think of this guy? If he's dealing in poison,
he goes down with everyone else."

Tricia sat with her ankle crossed over her knee and
picked at a thread hanging from the cuff of her jeans.
"He likes to size people up, I guess. He's tough but fair
and he wants these people, General Hadley most of all."

An alarm bell rang in the computer and Travis sat forward quickly flicking to the GPS screen. The week before he'd noticed Hadley drove the latest Caddy off the
line. So that night he'd taken a little midnight run, past
the little general's house. A peek inside had told him all
he'd needed to know. The Caddy had all the bells and
whistles, including a fully operational GPS system. It
had taken only minutes to shimmy under his car and pig-
gyback an AdVance beacon to the factory system. And
now the tracker was playing his tune.

"You wanted to do something. Hadley's on the
move." He stood and fished the keys to his Firebird out
of his pocket and tossed them to Trish. "You drive. I'll
ride shotgun and play navigator," he said unplugging the
laptop from its charger. "Let's see what the little general's up to."

They were in the car and on the way to intercept
Hadley in less than a minute. He was traveling west on
Interstate 24 by the time they got on the same highway
heading east. Then he turned south onto Academy Boulevard. "Go south on Twenty-first Street. It'll be coming up on the right," he directed Tricia.

He studiously avoided looking at the speedometer. There'd be little sense handing Trish the keys to a car and not expecting excess speed. "I'm there," she called out, and he braced for a high-speed turn. "What's he doing now?"

"Still on Academy headed south. If he's on his way to play golf at Broadmoor, I'll spit," Travis told her.

Trish laughed. "Wouldn't that look great on my report? Tailed suspect to an afternoon of complete boredom."

"Hey, turn on Lake Circle. I think your report's going to be a little more interesting than that. He went south on Broadmoor Bluffs. Go straight when you get to Cheyenne Mountain Boulevard then head south at Broodmore Valley. If he heads east on Farthing we'll intercept him by turning down Star Ranch. Yep. There he goes. I think he's headed to NORAD."

"NORAD?" She sagged in her seat. "He must have some sort of contact here. That's got to be it! Ian had planned to come out here a week before he was killed. I remember seeing it on his calendar but it was scratched out as if he'd changed his mind. I don't think we should tail the general inside. Let's just get close enough to make sure that's where he's gone."

"What could Hadley be after here? Does his command have anything to do with NORAD?"

"General Fielding has General Hadley's wing working with the reservists who come to Peterson to train. Reservists have nothing to do with visits to NORAD. He could have a friend here and that's all this is about, but there's that appointment Ian changed his mind about. What if he didn't, Travis? What if he did come here and the Bucs altered his calendar and stole his notes after they killed him? What if whoever General Hadley's here to see was Ian's mistake?"

One of the things about this whole investigation that kept Travis awake at night was knowing she slept, alone and vulnerable, on that base. And in the same kind of apartment Harrison nearly died in. The same base where Ian Kelly was murdered. "Then I guess we don't follow him any further. I think the time has come for another night of B and E. What are his rights as far as his home and office again?"

"He has the right to expect privacy at home. But his office belongs to the Air Force. We can search it with permission from his employer."

Travis tapped his fingers on the door panel. "Okay. Then I don't think this trip can be our reason for asking permission. I put the tracker on his car at his residence. Following Taylor to the general's office with the drugs, however, *is* probable cause…in the civilian sector at least."

"In military circles, too. Besides which, I ran this idea past General Fielding. He's considering it. We've exhausted all the other avenues we had unless we wait for another shipment to come in. We can follow it, but the sheer size of the duffel Edwards and Taylor handed over bothers me. That could have been as much as…fifty kilos." She said the amount with a faraway tone as if she'd remembered something that bothered her.

Travis narrowed his eyes, considering her. She

looked really upset. "Is something wrong? Did you remember something else from Kelly's notes?"

She shook her head but still looked worried. Maybe
breaking into the general's office had her spooked. They
had come close to getting caught and she'd been the vulnerable one hanging out on the beam. "Look, I know the
last time was pretty hairy and we didn't want to go tipping our hand, but I think this is our only option."

She nodded and took a deep breath. "Me, too. Let's
call General Fielding. I can't stand the thought of that
much more coke flooding the area. There's a new moon
tonight." She whipped the Firebird around and started
back the way they'd come.

Travis mentally rubbed his hands together. It would
be a perfect night for a little search-and-destroy mission.
They'd search the office and, with the Lord's help, maybe
they'd be able to destroy the two organizations that were
dealing death and destruction to the citizens of Colorado.

Tricia stepped out the back door of her apartment into
the crisp, clear, moonless night. Travis followed; like
her, he'd dressed in the same black turtleneck and pants
as they'd worn for the hangar incursion. A pass key instead of her lock pick set was nestled in her pocket and
cut way down on the possibility of getting caught by the
SPs at General Hadley's door. She had a penlight in her
pocket and her AFOSI ID was ready for inspection if
they were stopped.

They walked hand in hand like a couple out for an
evening stroll at just about nine, a respectable time to

be out and about and not attract attention. After she used the pass key, they slipped into the T-shaped building undetected. General Hadley's office was on the first floor at the end of a long hall and the intersection of two short ones. They crept along it, three bright red Exit signs providing all the illumination they needed. All was quiet as she unlocked the outer office door, then a nearly undetectable beam of light flashed beyond the secretary's desk in Hadley's office. Startled, Tricia pulled the door closed and motioned Travis toward the first office door along the side hall. She quickly unlocked it and stepped in. Travis followed.

"What?" he whispered.

"Someone's in his office already."

"Hadley? In the dark?"

"Not the general. Searching it, I think. I saw the beam of a penlight."

The sound of Hadley's office door opening tempted her. She had to know who'd been in there. So she cracked the door. Travis step behind her, his arm raised, his weapon ready. And Max Vance closed the general's door and crept down the hall, his agile movement erasing a decade from his tally of years.

Enough light leaked in that Tricia could see Travis's outline as he moved to the window, smoothly replacing his weapon into the holster at his back. He lifted one of the blind slats, silently watching.

What was he thinking? What would she say to him?

He dropped the slat and moved toward her a minute or two later.

"Travis," she whispered, putting a hand on his forearm. His muscles were tense to the consistency of granite.

"Let's get this done and get out of here," he said. His tone told her to leave it alone. He needed time.

Well, of course he needs time. His hero just took a deadly dive off a mile-high pedestal.

Tricia snapped a quick nod and opened the door. He could have all the time he needed, and if continuing on with the night's mission helped, then so much the better. It was time to end this.

Once again she gained access to General Hadley's outer office. They moved swiftly through then another quick unlock put them in the inner sanctum of the Buccaneers' fearless leader. Travis wasted no time and moved to the computer behind the general's desk. She started searching for anything that might be incriminating.

She moved from a filing cabinet to bookshelves but then looked over at the desk. At Travis, whose features were illuminated by the computer screen. The look on his face reminded her of fire and ice—remote and furious at the same time. Then a wicked little grin tipped his lips up at one corner. "Gotcha, you self-serving son of—"

"Got him how?" she insisted, moving across the room to him. Was this it? Had they cracked the case this easily after all the watching and waiting.

"I just got through to his private e-mail account. I'm assuming since I'm accessing through a government computer that whatever I find is admissible."

"Definitely," she said, and laid her hand on his shoulder.

It seemed almost by instinct that he covered her hand with his and pressed it against him. She almost breathed a sigh of relief. He didn't blame her.

"Well, he's got a pen pal in Venezuela," he said, still working quickly, his fingers flying over the keyboard.

Tricia watched for a moment as Travis scanned the e-mails for information, then started on the desk. She opened a drawer and accidentally dropped her penlight. The metal struck the wooden bottom and made a hollow sound, drawing even Travis's glance.

"What have we here?" she asked, running her hands along the seams till she found a finger hole.

"I hope it's as good as what I just came up with. This message expressly ties Hadley, the Buccaneers and his Diablo contact to La Mano Oscura. Apparently Diablo's ringleader hasn't been entirely forthcoming with La Mano Oscura's payments. The pilots are getting antsy about facing down the drug lord. Unfortunately, Hadley only refers to him as *El Patrón.* Hadley's warning the Diablo leader that he needs full payment for the next shipment. But it doesn't look as if they're equals in this. His tone's a little too deferential and he's also not using this guy's *name,* either." To her ears, Travis's tone said he was furious at his father and wanted to be the one responsible for bringing him down. She wasn't sure if that was a good idea for him psychologically or not but it was the way it was and there was little she could do to change that now.

Travis switched to another message as she set down the box that had formed the false bottom. "Here Hadley says he didn't like having to take the chance of stealing the KH to put *El Patrón* off. KH," he muttered, deep in thought.

At that moment the drawer yielded the answer to Travis's unspoken question. She pulled out a CD with "KH" written on the jewel case and leaned over to show it to him. "KH as in Key Hole Satellite imaging."

"That's the real high-definition stuff the rest of us in the field would just love to get our hands on, right?"

"And apparently so would a drug lord. Imagine how easy he would have it staying ahead of the authorities. Talk about inside information. I'd lay bets this is what General Hadley was doing out at NORAD. He doesn't have this kind of clearance but someone in NORAD would."

Travis pulled a CD out of his jacket pocket and slid it into the computer. The soft whir of the machine quickly filled the room. "Maybe with Hadley and the Bucs in custody, one of them will rat out their superiors. Especially with this evidence staring them in the face," he added, pulling the CD out and tapping the case on the desktop.

She stared down at the CD in her hand. "In the meantime, I can't chance alerting the general that we were here by taking this. I also can't stand to risk KH Satellite images getting to a drug lord before we round them all up."

Travis took the CD from her and stared at it. Then he started going though the drawers. In seconds he came up with an identical CD from a stack in a bottom drawer.

"You gotta love the military. They probably have the same supplier at Space Com that they have over here." He switched the two. "There you go. *El Patrón,* whoever he may be, gets a nice blank CD." Again that dark wicked grin appeared as he passed her the CD he'd copied. "I wonder if this week's pilot can talk himself out of this one with *El Patrón.*"

She very much doubted any of those involved were going to be able to talk themselves out of the evidence they'd come up with that night, and seeing the determination in Travis's eyes, Max Vance had less chance of it than anyone.

Chapter Nineteen

"I'm so sorry about your father, Trav," Tricia said as they walked along toward her house.

Travis shivered and hunched his shoulders against the chilly air. He sincerely wanted to break something. "He's the one who'll be sorry when I get through with him. Sam tried to tell him but he obviously didn't listen."

Tricia grabbed his arm and pulled him to a halt. "You and your brother knew what he was up to?"

"Sam saw him talking to Barclay one day. Barclay is up to something and Sam worried that Dad was up to *his* old tricks again. He told him to cut it out so close to home. It's obvious he didn't listen." The look on her face was one of abject horror. "Wait a minute. What exactly did you see back there?"

"Tonight? Not much. But then this isn't the first time I saw him incriminating himself. After that I tried to find out about him. His past is this strange record of a military man whose career went nowhere for too many years and who never took his family with him no matter where he was stationed. And then there's the implication of a house way too nice for his pay grade. I didn't *want* to believe he was involved in this, but I couldn't dismiss the possibility. I figured I'd protect you and Sam from suspicion of a cover-up by keeping what I knew and saw to myself. Then I overheard him on the phone in his office on the tenth talking about a fifty-kilo delivery."

Travis stared at her. His head was spinning. Noise roared though his head. Suddenly so much made sense. Fielding's insistence he work this investigation alongside of her just because they clashed in that alley. Her insistence, too. Fielding's odd comment that night at the restaurant about making sure they brought down Diablo's leader no matter who the man was. Her hesitation and odd reaction earlier today when she'd offhandedly estimated the number of kilos one of those duffel bags held.

She'd suspected his father all along. And Travis was only with her so she could watch him. He hadn't thought she could hurt him more than she had in the past.

He'd been wrong.

He clamped his lips tight, trying to slow his breathing. Why couldn't she have just left him dead inside? Why did she have to make him feel again? So he could feel the pain of her betrayal?

"Was I included in this investigation so you could watch me?" he demanded to know.

"General Fielding said—"

"*Was* I?" he repeated.

"Yes, but I—"

"*C-I-A* operatives," he said emphasizing each letter and refusing to listen to her excuses, "rarely, if ever, work a case close to home. That's what my father did all those years. If I'm angry at him for being there tonight, it's because he and the company broke their own unwritten rule. My father has spent his life in the service of this country. Maybe if you'd learned to trust people along with all the other changes you claim to have undergone over the years, you might not have gone chasing the wrong suspect. Maybe if you didn't judge every other man by your father, you'd have leveled with me and saved yourself the problem of putting up with me and my family all these weeks."

Unable to even look at her and her incredulous expression, he turned to walk away.

Once again she grabbed his arm. "Where are you going? Aren't you even going to let me explain," she demanded.

If there was heartbreak and panic in her voice, he refused to acknowledge it. He stared pointedly at his arm till she slowly released it. Then he answered. "No. I'm not going to listen. You had four weeks to talk to me. And, not that it's any of your business, but I'm going to see my criminal brother and father."

She glared at him. "You know, you haven't changed all that much, either. You still jump to conclusions and refuse to listen to explanations."

"*I* jump to conclusions? As far as I can see there is no explanation for doubting the integrity of me, my brother and my father. Or for spying on us in our own homes."

She blinked back what looked to be the beginning of tears. "I won't beg you to listen to me this time, Travis. If you can walk away this easily *again,* I guess what you're walking away from wasn't all that important to you after all. I need to call General Fielding and set up a meeting. The next flight probably takes off in the morning. Mitch Simpson's leave started at 2400."

Travis snapped a mocking salute. "Give my regards to Herr General. Happy promotion, Major. I hope you and the Air Force are very happy together."

Tricia stood there staring at him. With his heart heavy, Travis turned and walked away. Stunned nearly senseless by the depth of her betrayal, he somehow managed to put one foot in front of the other and got to where he'd left his car at the O Club. He looked up at the sky and laughed bitterly. In case the search went late, he hadn't wanted to damage her reputation by leaving his car sitting outside her place again. He hadn't wanted to cause her any career problems. For Tricia her career apparently really *was* everything.

Once he got to his car, Travis blasted out of the base and headed over to his parents' house with a full head of steam. Wasn't it bad enough that his father had missed almost his whole marriage? Did he have to endanger his wife by trying to stop international drug trafficking only miles from their house? More than anyone he should know that these South Americans played rough and often took out whole families for revenge and to send messages.

He found his father in his study. "Where's Mom?" he demanded.

Max looked up, obviously surprised by the tone. "She's over at Fiona's experimenting on some recipes. Why?"

"Because you may not care about Mom or what effect the job has had on her but I do."

His father stood slowly behind his desk. "Watch it, Travis."

"Funny choice of words. You see I *watched* you come out of Hadley's office tonight. And Tricia saw you with him one other time. I don't know all of what you're up to and I don't care. But you'd better back off before Mom or Lucia get caught in the cross fire."

"No, it's *you* who doesn't understand all that's at stake. I've had no choice. No choice at all in this. I promise your mother isn't in any danger, but I'm not at liberty to go into this further. If you're working on this with the Air Force, then please go careful out there. This is even more dangerous than it looks to even you. Is Sam involved, too?"

Still annoyed, Travis refused to answer. He just said goodbye and headed to Sam's. He had to give his brother the head's-up on what had happened. He put it out of his mind that Tricia was on her own out there meeting with Fielding and trying to decide where to go next.

Sam was outside his house waiting. "Dad called. I hear you really tore into him."

"Tricia and I went into Hadley's office tonight. Dad was inside when we arrived."

Sam whistled. "I thought he might be working again. I told you that, right? That must have been interesting for you. Did you tell Tricia about Dad's previous and maybe current employer?"

Travis stuffed his hands in his front pockets. "Not until she gave me *her* theory. She's been playing all of us. It seems she saw Dad in some mysterious meeting with her chief suspect. She tried to find out about his past. Since then, Dad's been under suspicion of being Diablo's ringleader."

"Dad? Our career company man father?" Sam hooted. "That's too funny. What did she say when you eased her mind?"

"Eased her mind? She thought we'd cover up for him. She thought he was selling drugs to kids!"

Sam groaned. "Tell me you didn't do something stupid like break off your relationship with her." Travis glared. "You did! Over a little hurt pride and a misunderstanding about Dad and his mysterious movements around town? Bro, I saw him with Barclay and wondered what he was up to talking to that sleazy dude. Think, will you? What would these meetings look like to someone who tried to investigate our father?"

Travis stared at Sam. What had Tricia said? Something about protecting them by keeping silent. What *had* she meant by that?

His cell phone rang and he looked at the number. It was Trish.

Forty minutes after Travis stormed off, Trish turned the corner near her house and found she could hardly see. She was blinded by tears. She'd gone out running after setting up the meeting with General Fielding. She'd hoped the run would clear her head but she'd given up half a mile into the run. She couldn't see where she was running for her tears.

Over and over she replayed the confrontation in her head and couldn't think of a better way to say what she'd needed to say. The truth was he hadn't heard her and that was because she'd messed up so bad. But Travis had messed up, too. He hadn't listened to her. She'd done what she had to do. Her job. Her duty. She'd had no choice.

But, Lord, why did it have to end like this? He's *hurt.* I'm *hurt. Why did we have to lose each other?*

She gave up fighting this newest wave of tears a block from the apartment and let them flow. That was her second big mistake of the night. Because when she got to her house, she didn't see the man in the shadows. And when she opened her car door, wiping the wetness from her cheeks, the cold steel of a revolver pressing against her neck was her first warning of danger.

Before her mind had fully processed his presence at her side, he grabbed her by the throat and pressed the gun harder against her.

"Don't try anything, Major. Where's the boyfriend?"

"Not with me, obviously," she croaked.

He let the pressure up a bit. "You aren't even going to pretend confusion over why I came after you, are you?"

She couldn't believe how calm she was. How centered and clear-headed. Since finding the Lord, death hadn't held much of a sting, but she'd always been a little apprehensive about how she'd leave the world. Now that it was here and she had little choice, she knew only one regret: that Travis didn't understand how much she loved him or why she'd kept silent.

"Would it do any good to pretend I don't understand what you're about?" she asked.

"No. You were in my office tonight. I forgot something and went back for it. And I saw you and your boyfriend leaving. Then I saw you argue. I set Walters and Rule on him. They'll be waiting when he gets home. I decided to take care of you myself because my other resources were drunk as skunks at the officers' club."

Travis. They'd gone after Travis. A picture of Ian's body flashed in her mind. She couldn't think about Travis like that. Not now. Not imagine the worst and still function. She had to get away. Had to warn him.

"Aren't you going to beg for your life?"

"Did Ian?" she asked, her mind trying to sort through every possible scenario that might get her free of General Hadley and that weapon he was carrying.

"Kelly, beg? No. But I understand Harrison did. Kelly was an arrogant so-and-so but you had to respect him."

"Death was no big deal for Ian. He knew better things were waiting for him. By the way, I won't be doing any begging, either. Sorry to spoil your fun."

I know You're waiting for me, Lord, but I can't give up yet. I have to save Travis. And I don't want him feeling guilty that he left me alone if he outsmarts them. So how do I buy time? And how do I get away so I can warn him?

Then it came to her. "I'd like to point out, though," she told the general, "that sound travels pretty far around here. You pull that trigger and you won't get the time to ditch your uniform this time when I bleed all over you."

"Do you take me for a fool? We're going for a little ride to where it'll be nice and lonely."

"I have to tell you, George, you're a walking cliché," she chided, hoping to get him flustered and careless.

Instead she got cold anger. He pressed the gun harder against her carotid artery. His message was clear. He didn't have to shoot her if she passed out. He was in control. "Close your door," he ordered, keeping up the pressure.

She did as ordered and he let blood flow back into her head. She nearly did pass out as he dragged her backward and growled, "Get to the passenger side and get in. Now." His order told her three things. They were going somewhere, she'd be driving and unfortunately, he didn't underestimate her ability to outrun him.

Tricia kept watching for any little mistake that would let her break free. He didn't make any. Soon he'd shoved her in the front passenger door, forced her across the front seat and behind the wheel. "Head out Route Twenty-four to Twenty-sixth Street. Then go south. Lots of nice woodlands out that way to dump a body." Tricia instinctively stiffened and he chuckled. It was the sound of pure evil having a high old time. "Was that indelicate of me?" he asked.

"Probably closer to cruel," she muttered.

He ignored her and added, "Get going and keep your hands on the wheel."

So far he'd only mentioned Ian and Harrison. She was tempted to tell him all his crimes had been found out but she decided to keep that in reserve to throw him later if she needed the distraction. And right then she didn't want to anger him further. She was batting a thousand on that score, she thought, remembering how angry Travis was with her. Tears once again pooled in her eyes. But as if being given the solution to her dilemma, thinking of Travis gave her the answer she needed.

She'd called him from her car after leaving his place earlier before they rendezvoused at her apartment to walk to General Hadley's office. She'd wanted to remind him to bring some blank CD-R's to copy the general's data files if they managed to hack their way in. Which meant her cell phone, which lay between her and General Hadley next to her seat belt, had his number ready for dialing. By some miracle the general hadn't seen it. All she had to do was get her hand down there and press the call button, then push it onto the floor behind her before he saw it. And say another prayer that it wouldn't fall on the disconnect button and end the call before it began.

"The guard's going to stop us at the gate if we don't buckle up," she told General Hadley.

"Why would you warn me?" he asked cagily.

"Because the SP on the gate is about twenty-two and has a young baby. If he stops us, you'll kill him. You've created enough orphans these past few weeks."

"Fine. Then buckle up."

She might have been able to get away while he stretched the belt across his girth but it was only a slim chance. If she failed, there'd be no one to warn Travis, and that kid on the gate really would become another casualty. He'd see a general and hesitate just long enough to lose his life. But if she used General Hadley's slight distraction to dial her phone, she might be able to warn Travis and both their chances would be that much greater.

She hit the button as the general snapped the belt together and shoved the phone through the opening to the back seat under the tucked-away armrests. Then waited a beat or two for Travis to hopefully answer. If only she could know the call was still connected.

"Ouch," she said, to cover any sound coming from the phone, "I pinched myself in the seat belt."

"You're going to have more than a little pinch to worry about soon enough, Major. You don't seem to be taking your situation very seriously."

"I take my impending death very seriously, General Hadley. You've sent two men to kill the man I love and you're forcing me to drive out…where exactly *are* we going for my execution?"

"You're a gutsy broad. I'll give you that."

Tricia nearly laughed. She was shaking in her jogging shoes but showing this man her fear would only weaken her resolve to get out of this.

"If you think so highly of me, do me the courtesy of telling me where my final resting place will be."

"Bear Creek Canyon Park. That's always been such a tongue twister. I sort of fancy hearing all about your remains being found and listening to those news anchors trying to get that mouthful out fast and smooth."

"I didn't know you were such a funny guy, George. I just might laugh myself to death."

Please be hearing this, Travis. Please be safe.

Chapter Twenty

Travis heard Trish's voice already chatting to someone else when he answered the phone. He almost hung up, thinking she'd mistakenly punched her redial button during her meeting with General Fielding. Then the topic of the muffled conversation chilled him.

"I take my impending death very seriously, General Hadley," she was saying. "You've sent two men to kill the man I love and you're forcing me to drive out…where exactly *are* we going for my execution?"

Travis heart ached with pain and fear for her but he knew he had to put his pain aside. He grabbed Sam and dragged his head next to the phone so he could hear. So he could help.

"You're a gutsy broad. I'll give you that," Hadley said.

"If you think so highly of me, do me the courtesy of telling me where my final resting place will be."

"Bear Creek Canyon Park. That's always been such a tongue twister. I sort of fancy hearing all about your remains being found and listening to those news anchors trying to get that mouthful out fast and smooth."

"I didn't know you were such a funny guy, George. I just might laugh myself to death."

Travis winced and hit the mute button to cut down on the chance Hadley would figure out what Tricia had done. "Watch it, Trish," he whispered as Sam stepped away and pulled his own cell phone off his hip.

Travis knew Trish after all the time they'd spent together working this month—had it only been a month? He knew her warrior heart and he was sure the phone call was no accident. And her own safety was irrelevant to her. She'd done this primarily to keep *him* safe and to tell him she loved him. Only now was she trying to feed him information—just in case he was listening. That she might think he would refuse to pick up the call made his heart ache all the more. *Give me a chance to make this right, Lord. Don't let her die because I'm an idiot.*

"I'll call my captain," Sam said as they both moved toward the house. "He can coordinate a mop-up at your house. Thank God you left Cody here earlier tonight. From what you've said, those two would have killed him without blinking an eye."

Travis stared at his brother, his heart in his throat. Hadley would kill Trish. "Yeah. And you're right. They would, and Hadley would kill Trish just as easily. But our good fortune may be Hadley's downfall. I think it's time to put Cody's training to good use."

"How you want to handle this? Just you, me and Cody?" Sam asked.

As if on cue Cody woofed at the door and Travis nodded then jogged ahead to let him out. "You drive, Sam," he said, holding the door open. "Get your gun and I'll boot up my computer. We should be able to get to the park first then close to wherever he makes her stop. I put a GPS tracker on Trish's car. It's about to pay off."

Travis had his weapon unlocked and holstered and the computer booted by the time Sam barreled back out of the house. Jessica called out a promise of prayer then ducked back inside as his brother threw himself behind the wheel. Sam was a lucky man to know his woman was home safe. It was Travis's own fault he wasn't in the same position.

"I left her, Sam. I left her on that base where I knew they got to Kelly and Harrison. I'm such a prize idiot!"

Sam shot him a look as he pulled out onto Goldmine Lane. "You aren't getting an argument from me."

Travis hooked the cell phone up to its speaker just as the silence in Tricia's car ended with the general complaining about her driving and threatening to shoot her then and there if she didn't slow down.

"I'm coming, sweetheart," Travis muttered. "Just slow down and go careful. Don't rile him anymore."

He'd no sooner said that when Tricia snickered. "Are you a white-knuckled flyer, too? No wonder they passed you over on the past couple promotion go-rounds."

"I didn't know you were this annoying or I'd have brought along some duct tape," the general fumed.

"Is that why you did it? Getting passed over must have really rankled."

"I gave my life to the Air Force. And that's how they thanked me. You bet that's why I did it. I corrupted some of their best pilots." He laughed. "Took them over to the darker side."

"You're a regular Darth Vader, aren't you?"

"She's going to get her fool head blown off!" Sam warned.

"So what are Captains Taylor and Edwards so busy celebrating that you couldn't trust them to take care of me?"

Travis fumbled for the pocket recorder in his glove box. "I think she's trying to get him to admit to whatever she can and implicate the others with us as witnesses."

"After the way you wiped the floor up with Mitch Simpson?" Hadley answered after a pause. "I don't think sending Edwards and Taylor up against you would have been smart. Those two aren't quite as big as their egos. Besides, it was more than a few drinks. They were celebrating. Turn left onto Twenty-first."

"So what were they celebrating? Did your boss finally pay up to *El Patrón*?"

General Hadley didn't answer right away. "I'm my own boss," he said at last. "Take the next right. That'll take us into the park."

"Okay," Travis told Sam, "that puts them on Gold Camp. Stick to Twenty-sixth up ahead here. They intersect later on. Do you think you can follow them with your lights off when they pass in front of us on Gold Camp?"

"Can do. We'll get her out of this. Believe that."

As Travis nodded, Tricia made the right and said,

"You know you have a boss, George. He runs the Diablo syndicate in town."

"Oh…you *are* good. I seriously underestimated you, Major. I thought you were just on to me and my pilots for Kelly's murder. We got rid of all his evidence against us for the drug running. So Harrison did rat out us out for the drugs. We thought it was just for Kelly's murder."

"He did neither," came Tricia's tight reply. "He was a suspect and I was trying to decide if an old friend was in on your schemes or just not noticing. You did what you did to him for no reason at all. I'd been on to you already for weeks because you missed a note in Ian's pocket."

"A note? What note?"

"The one that linked La Mano Oscura and Diablo for all of us."

Hadley cursed and Travis wanted to. Sam was right. She was pushing Hadley too hard and they were in spitting distance of the park.

"Oh, and by the way," she added, turning the screws to everyone's nerves. "Travis isn't just a P.I. He's a computer whiz. You didn't protect your secrets from him, George. You don't mind my calling you, George, I hope. I've always wanted to be on a first-name basis with a general. Since you're about to kill me, this is my last chance. It seems only fair you'd oblige me."

"She's making me crazy, bro," Sam said.

Him, too. "He can't kill her while they're moving," Travis said just as Tricia's car swung onto the road in front of them. Sam moved out, following at a distance behind the overbright taillights.

"She's riding her brake," Sam pointed out. "Maybe she knows we're here."

"She doesn't know, Sam. For all she knows, I never answered because it was her."

Cody, who had been as quiet as he'd ever been suddenly sat up and poked his head between the seats. The dog's ears twitched and he whined. He either sensed the increased tension in the car or he'd caught Trish's scent. Travis reached up and patted his strong canine shoulder. "Yeah, fella. That's our girl up ahead and she's in big trouble. You've got to hush, Cody. Hush," he ordered, then rolled down his window.

Keeping his eyes trained on the computer screen, Travis watched the movement of the car as Sam let the distance stretch out a little. When no movement translated to the screen for several seconds, Travis heart pounded even harder. "They stopped," he told his brother, and two shots echoed through the forest. Sam floored the Firebird and the game little car leaped forward.

Though she'd been waiting for the moment, Tricia was mildly surprised and completely terrified when General Hadley put the gun to her head and turned the ignition switch off. The car slowed.

"Now we'll take a little walk, you'll kneel down and I put a bullet in that smart brain of yours. I understand you'll never feel a thing."

Please, Lord, let Travis be out there. Safe, at least, if he couldn't be here to help me. Forgive my stupidity

*about his father. Let him forgive me and himself and go
on without guilt.*

Her hands shaking, Tricia gripped the wheel. "So I
guess we're getting out." She really hated that her
voice shook.

Give me courage, Lord.

"Are you following me out, or am I following you?"
she asked, looking straight ahead, feeling oddly resigned to her own death. The car lights were still lit, il-
luminating the thick forest ahead. The car sat still but
she'd left it in drive. A slightly steep ditch lay to the right
of the car.

An idea struck her then and she understood the calm.
She wasn't supposed to stop fighting for herself and for
a life with Travis. She thanked God for the insight and
the passive-restraint seat belts on her car. They were attached to her door and not the floor so the doors could
open without unlatching the belts. She might not get
completely away but she still had a chance.

"I'm following you out and don't try anything," General Hadley said, his seat belt still buckled nice and
tight. He'd have to undo his then hers or get out his own
door if she bailed out.

"You're in charge," she said, then popped open the
door. He reached to grab her arm but she was already
moving. She hit the light switch, plunged them into
darkness and twisted toward the ground as fast as she
could. She dove back toward the rear of the car and a
bullet slammed into her door as the springs in the seat
belt pulled it shut. Scrambling toward the back of the

car, she felt another bullet punch through the back door, barely missing her head. She rolled to her feet, ripped off her light-colored jacket as she ran, hoping distance and shadows would throw off his aim, giving her a chance.

The Firebird screeched around the bend and caught Tricia and Hadley in the glare of the headlights. They were both in the middle of the narrow road. The general took aim but she ran in a zigzag pattern. Hadley couldn't know which way she'd go next but then neither could Travis. Hadley's shot whizzed past Tricia and slammed into the Firebird.

"Tricia's in my line of fire," he told Sam.

"Hold on," Sam shouted, and put the car into a sideways skid partially facing Travis's door up road. Travis threw open his door, shouting, "Get him," to Cody. The shepherd launched out of the car just as Hadley took aim once again. Cody hit him full throttle with all his hundred-plus pounds but a shot still sliced through the air.

And Trish spun and crumpled to the asphalt.

Travis's heart stopped as he ran for all he was worth only yards behind Cody. He dropped to the ground next to Tricia and time, which had seemed to slow to half speed, stopped altogether.

The Firebird's headlights pointed away from where she lay but there was enough spill-over light that Travis could see blood, black as death, pooling beneath her side. He was afraid to touch her. Afraid to find out. *Please, dear Jesus, don't let us be too late. Don't let me lose her now.*

Then she groaned and it was the sweetest sound he'd ever heard. "I must be alive," she whispered. "I wouldn't hurt in heaven, would I? That just wouldn't be fair." She opened dark mahogany eyes and gazed up at him. "And I'm not sure angels frown like that, either."

"I don't have a lot to smile about. I almost lost my best girl," he told her, his voice even less steady than hers. "Let me take a look at what we've got here," Travis said, hearing Sam shout, "Guard," to Cody at the same time. The snarling growls he'd barely been aware of quieted a bit but not completely.

Carefully peeling Trish's sweatshirt up and rolling her torn slacks down a bit, Travis exposed the wound at her waist. He sucked a deep breath, desperately trying not to react and scare her. He was terrified enough for both of them. The skin had been laid open by the path of the bullet but there wasn't enough light to see more than blood and torn tissue. He pulled a clean handkerchief from his pocket and applied pressure, his heart wrenching at her agonized gasp.

"Call." Travis's voice broke and came out as barely a whisper. He took a deep breath and tried again. "Call an ambulance," he shouted to his brother as he checked her pulse. It wasn't very strong.

Sam walked the few feet to stand at his side. "Done. I did that after I disarmed Hadley. Cody's guarding him. Neither one looks happy about it. Hadley's petrified and Cody really wants a piece of him."

"He's not the only one," Travis muttered, making Trish smile sleepily.

"Captain Sullivan says they got the two at your house, bro. And an ambulance is on the way. How you doin', Tricia?"

"It hurts to get shot. Did you know that?" she asked, sounding fuzzier by the minute. Her skin was getting cold and clammy and the pulse under his fingertips was getting faster and faster.

"I'll take your word for it, thank you very much," Sam teased, trying to lighten the moment.

But Travis found nothing funny at that point. Trish's pulse was so fast he was sure she was in shock. He dragged off his jacket and Sam did the same and covered her with them before fading away to handle Hadley. Cody came over then, whimpering and wanting to help. So Travis had him snuggle up next to her to help keep her warm.

Tricia didn't seem to notice. "Are we all right?" she asked. As dark as it was, he could see tears roll from the corners of her eyes.

"Shh," he ordered, an ambulance siren wailing in the background. "We're fine. Sam reminded me what an idiot I am. I'm so sorry I wasn't there for you. That I didn't listen." There was so many other things he wanted to say to her but not with Hadley handcuffed only a few feet away.

"Trav, keep this…a secret." She blinked, trying to focus. "CDs in my toilet tank."

Travis didn't care about the case at that moment but he could see Tricia was trying to tell him something that her mind was too confused to reason out.

"Celebrating. They were celebrating. Why?" she asked.

To calm her down, he asked Sam to stow the general out of sight before the ambulance got there so no one would see who the suspect was. It wouldn't do for word to get out about the general's arrest before they could set a trap for his local partner and his Venezuelan connection. Sam had no sooner stashed the general and moved the Firebird from the middle of the road than the ambulance arrived.

"Give General Hadley to your father," she whispered.

"Right," he agreed. He'd have agreed to anything. "Maybe we can all get together later and brainstorm this with him," he suggested to keep her calm. "But first we're going to take care of you and get you to Memorial."

Chapter Twenty-One

Tricia crossed her arms and glared at Travis. It was the first time she'd seen him since she'd been treated, and he looked like a bear with a thorn in his paw. But she wasn't fooled by the scowl or the indignation. He was a teddy bear.

"I am not staying in this hospital tonight, Travis Vance." She looked at Dr. Adam Montgomery. He was Travis's oldest friend and now she needed him as an ally. "Adam, you said it was just a graze wound and that all I needed was stitches and antibiotics for two weeks. You stitched me up. The nurse said you can supply me with the first three doses of antibiotics and painkillers until I can get a prescription filled tomorrow. Is there really any reason I have to stay all night? And when you answer, look at me, not Mr. Strong, Silent and Cranky over there. Is there really any reason to admit me?"

Adam grimaced and she knew she'd won. "I'm sorry, Travis. She's not in shock anymore. Her pulse is great. I wouldn't normally keep her. People feel better at home. Get better faster." He shot his friend a crooked grin. "Of course, I don't usually get hysterical calls from boyfriends ordering me to come and operate on someone not in need of surgery, either."

"What do you call all those stitches?" Travis demanded. "And all that blood. She must have lost a gallon."

Montgomery chuckled. "She never had a gallon, and those stitches wouldn't challenge a second-year resident. Relax, your girl's just fine. Take her home to Lidia and let your mother fuss over her." He looked back to Tricia and smiled. "Don't do too much. Get lots of rest. No work. Tell your boss to call me if he has a problem with that. I'll see you in my office in two weeks to take a look at the stitches. The nurse will give you wound care instructions and a list of problems I'd want to hear about. Take care and good night." With that, white coat flapping around jean-clad legs, he left before Travis could protest.

Travis huffed out a deep breath, shaking his head. "Okay. I'll tell the nurse she can come in and help you get dressed."

He left after one more long lingering look at her. The nurse helped her dress, gave her the instructions and list of symptoms to watch for and pronounced her free to leave. Travis greeted her in the E.R. hall, taking her hand and still looking way too concerned. "They just let you leave? Not even a wheelchair? What's happening around this hospital?"

"I'm fine. Let's just get going before all this nice novocaine wears off, okay?"

Sam walked up to them near the doors to the parking lot. He looked nearly as troubled as Travis but he was looking at his brother. "I hate to tell you this but Dad just called. There's a meeting set for tonight." He looked at his watch. "Well, midnight just came and went so make that this morning. We're all expected."

Travis sighed. "Will this night never end? We'll drop Trish at Mom and Dad's so I know there's someone with her, then we'll get going. Where's the meeting?"

Tricia was about to protest that she had no intention of missing a meeting of this importance when Sam settled the argument before it got started. "Mom and Dad's." At Travis's blank look Sam added. "The *meeting* is at Mom and Dad's. The powers that be are trying to keep the arrests under wraps, as Tricia suggested. That precludes meeting on the base or at the station or anywhere that might arouse suspicion that something big's going down."

Travis scowled. "So Dad volunteered their house?"

Sam gestured toward a silver Mercedes—Max Vance's car. "Actually, it was Mom's idea, along with sending me here in Dad's car. She didn't want Tricia getting bounced around in any of our vehicles or needing to go somewhere else. Or being excluded. You should have heard the explosion over that suggestion. I'm just glad I didn't make it. I think Dad was already in hot water with her over some part of this business, and after Vesuvius erupted, he gave in. Neither of them is saying what's going on between them but I've got to think using their house is a good idea."

"It sounds like the best place, Trav," Tricia agreed as he opened the door for her and helped her get settled in the luxurious back seat. She grabbed his arm to get his undivided attention. "You said it yourself. Not even your family knew what your father did all those years. And I don't think it will put your mother or sister in any danger."

Travis pursed his lips then finally nodded. He closed her door and walked around the back of the car and surprised her by climbing in next to her instead of up front with Sam. "Who'll be at the meeting?" he asked Sam as soon as he settled.

"Me, my DEA contact Greg Carvell, Dad, General Fielding, Jake Montgomery, you and Tricia." Sam chuckled. "And, knowing Dad, I imagine there'll be some spooks in the bushes."

"And Mom serving coffee, cannoli and biscotti." Travis snickered, obviously finding humor in that possibility. "This ought to be good."

Tricia laughed but a stitch in her side pulled and she thought better of it. She was suddenly more than grateful for the suspension in the Mercedes. Sam also laughed at Travis's assessment but Travis had noticed her grimace of pain. He moved closer and she rested her head on his shoulder.

"This meeting may become Company legend. Mom and the CIA. Incredible," Sam said, looking back at them through the rearview mirror.

"Where are General Hadley and the pilots?" Tricia wondered.

"Mitchell Simpson is still on base and sleeping like a baby. Taylor and Edwards found themselves being yanked into a dark van when they stepped out of the Officers' Club at around eleven. Well, actually I hear it was more like they staggered out. They were taken to spend some time with Rule and Walters and some Company baby-sitters. Hadley is at a different location but no less out of circulation. I understand Fielding's with him right now."

Tricia put her hand in Travis's, enjoying the moments of closeness even in the midst of what amounted to a briefing. "Have you heard why no one picked up Mitch Simpson?" she asked.

Sam shrugged and Travis caressed her cheek with his free hand. "Maybe they want him to make the flight for some reason," he guessed. "Try not to worry so much. It'll all work out."

But she couldn't seem to stop trying to work out a way to salvage her last Air Force investigation. *Wait a minute. Last investigation? Where had that come from?* But the answer was there under her head—a strong shoulder to lean on in tough times. It was there in the unconscious caress of his gentle hand telling her she was cherished. And it was there in the corded muscles of the arm next to hers—arms that offered solace and the kind of strength that would never turn on her.

She couldn't leave Travis and her love for him behind. She couldn't give up on the possibility of a life together. And she couldn't expect him to leave Colorado Springs and his wonderful family and friends for the whims of the Air Force. That meant this *was* her last investigation.

So, decision made, she turned her mind to the problem at hand, wanting to salvage all she could after all that had gone wrong. "Letting the flight go forward *would* keep what happened tonight under wraps, but Mitch Simpson has to check in with General Hadley before he takes off," she pointed out. "When the general isn't there in the morning…"

Travis squeezed her hand. "We'll find out what the higher-ups have in mind when we get there."

Max and Lidia Vance were sitting in the den when they arrived. Travis's mother rushed to Tricia and took charge, generally making her feel cosseted and cared for in a way she never had been by her own mother. Lidia had already found a loose forest-green velour T-shirt-style dress in the back of her closet that she'd bought for Lucia but that her firefighter daughter had refused to wear. She also produced a pair of Lucia's slippers to wear in lieu of the jogging shoes that had seen better days.

Together they devised a way for her to shower so Tricia felt cleaner at least when she walked back into the lounge. Still she was tired and sore, but when Travis's green eyes lit with joy when they fell on her, all her fatigue and most of her pain disappeared.

He stood and enfolded her in his arms. "You look a little better. Not strong enough for all this tonight but wonderful."

"Your mom gave me the dress. She says Lucia wouldn't wear it."

Travis chuckled and the sound echoed in his chest.

"Believe it. I haven't seen Lucia in a dress in years. Mom finally gave up. It looks pretty on you. How do you feel, really? No bravery."

"I took one of the painkillers." He looked so worried again that she grinned up at him, hoping to put him at ease. "It's your job to make sure I don't fall asleep with my face in one of your mother's cannoli."

Travis grinned back. "Will do, but you have to promise that if this gets to be too much, you'll go lie down." She nodded her promise. "Okay, then," he said. "The others are in the dining room. Fielding just got here and he looks like the cat that swallowed a flock of canaries."

"Then I guess we should go find out why he looks so pleased with himself."

They walked in holding hands and Travis refused to relinquish hers when she automatically went to raise her arm to salute.

"At ease. Sit down before you fall down, Major," General Fielding said. "You should be in bed."

Travis's eyebrows lifted. "I agree, but she's here now so let's get this over with so she can rest. I take it you're in charge?" he asked his father.

"C.J.," Max said, indicating the general, "and I agreed to dispense with any hierarchy nonsense. Several agencies and departments of the governments have been working different angles of the same problem. Those agencies and departments are represented here tonight. Most of us know some of the people at the table but not all. Let's introduce ourselves. I'm Max Vance and I've been doing a little consulting work on this situation."

Tricia noticed he never admitted to being CIA. The speaking glances exchanged between the Vance brothers told her she wasn't the only one who'd noticed.

"C. J. Fielding. I'm the base commander over at Peterson."

"Jake Montgomery. FBI computer expert."

A handsome man with golden-brown hair and even more golden eyes smiled at the group. "Greg Carvell, DEA."

She, Travis and Sam introduced themselves and Travis added, "Let's get this thing going so Trish can get the rest she deserves after what she's been through tonight."

"I can guarantee she'll also get the promotion she deserves for her part in cleaning up the mess Hadley helped create," General Fielding said, grinning fondly at her.

Blushing, Tricia kicked Travis under the table. He merely winked at her in return, shooting her a crooked grin. The man was incorrigible.

No wonder she loved him so much.

Chapter Twenty-Two

Travis sat back, intent on having as little to do as possible with the meeting. As far as he was concerned, he was there to watch Trish for signs of too much fatigue. But then C. J. Fielding grabbed his attention with the first words he spoke.

"In a secret raid a few minutes ago the FBI arrested and detained a man we believe is not only the Diablo syndicate leader in Colorado Springs but also its kingpin. Alistair Barclay has been using his network of hotels to distribute La Mano Oscura drugs here, throughout the country and around the world."

Sam slapped the desk. "I *knew* there was something dirty about that guy." He looked at their father. "Obviously, I wasn't alone."

"Are you the one who got this information, Mr. Vance?" Tricia asked.

"No." Max Vance shook his head. "I just didn't trust him or his business practices. He had too much ready cash and too aggressive a construction schedule. I really *was* trying to check him out only because he said he might run for mayor."

"Was your meeting with Hadley at the Air Force chapel official?" Tricia asked.

His father nodded. But it was Fielding who spoke up. "While you were being treated, Major, I met with Hadley. I told him Travis had made a tape of your conversation in the car. He confessed when I took the death penalty off the table in exchange for names and cooperation. He'll plead guilty to Major Kelly's murder, kidnapping, two counts of attempted murder and the trafficking charges. He'll never leave federal custody, of that I can assure you."

Max took over. "So, now we need to combine our separate pieces of information and decide on a coordinated strategy. As C.J. said earlier, it's time to cut the head off this snake. We have an operative in Venezuela trying to penetrate La Mano Oscura and learn the identity of *El Patrón*. Thus far he hasn't."

Fielding tossed the KH satellite CD they'd stolen from Hadley's office on the table. Then his father dropped a second CD onto the table in front of his place.

"Uh-oh. Which one of those did we steal and switch?" Travis asked, then held up his hand. That quick, he knew. He pointed to his father. "That's what you were doing there. You took the real one and substituted a fake. And we stole the fake and left a blank."

"No, actually I copied the KH to find out what's on it, and I left the original. That's what you two stole."

Travis grimaced. "Oh, man. Now what?"

"Now I'm thinking this may come together," Jake said, sitting straighter and making Travis feel a lot better. "I've been going through the copy you made of Hadley's files since Sam stopped by here with them earlier. I found a reference to a larger pickup in a bigger plane Hadley rented. They were going to be bringing five hundred kilos in the weekend of November thirteenth and a large exchange of money plus a large payment that Barclay had been holding back from *El Patrón* to cover all the Colorado Springs construction costs."

Carvell snapped his fingers, a sly grin blooming on his face. "Bingo. What if we make that flight ourselves? We could fill the plane with enough agents and firepower to take out *El Patrón's* main labs and cripple the man even if we can't get his name."

"Two things," Trish said. "How do we know where the labs are, and what do we do about the flight tomorrow? Well, no actually a third. Travis and I think there's a landing strip of some sort in the Yucatán. If that gets bypassed, our flight schedule might set off alarm bells in Venezuela."

His dad grinned and held up his KH CD. "One of the images on this baby is of an airstrip in Quintana Roo. Their lab is front and center in another image. When Hadley approached an old friend to buy KH images of sections of Venezuelan and the Yucatán, we found out and put someone in NORAD to watch for the exchange. It seemed to be a good guess Hadley was involved in something illegal. We didn't know what or how or when this disk was going out so I had to get in there tonight to get a look at it."

"I held off arresting Captain Simpson tonight," Fielding spoke up, "just in case we needed time to plan our next move before tonight's arrests become public knowledge. I think we should replace the KH CD and let Simpson take the flight." He held up the one Trish found in Hadley's office. "And then Sunday we arrest Simpson when he sets foot on the tarmac. All we have to do is put the KH in an envelope and leave it for Simpson with Hadley's secretary. She can blame his absence on an early golf meeting with me."

Travis noticed Tricia shifting uncomfortably in her chair. "I think you all can take it from here. Tricia is out on her feet and we've got nothing left to contribute." He stood. "So if you gentlemen will excuse us."

He hadn't given her much choice but Tricia stood, slid the notes she'd been making across to the general, nodded with a smile to the others and walked out.

Tricia turned as Travis slid the doors of the dining room closed on the meeting. "*That* was rude."

He grinned, completely unapologetic. "Yeah. But I could see you were getting tired and I wanted some time with you before you fade completely. It's still a pretty night. Let's go sit in the garden."

He put on his jacket and tossed a shawl that hung in the back hall over her shoulders. Holding her to his side with his arm slung across her shoulders, he led her out into the cool night and directed them to a stone bench near a small pond and a birdbath. It was hard to believe it had snowed a couple of weeks ago.

"The garden's lovely."

"Not half as lovely as you are." He fingered her hair and smiled. "There were so many things I wanted to say to you during that horrendous ride out to Bear Creek. Then when I finally got to you, you were hurt and Hadley was only a few feet away. That didn't seem like the right time." He straddled the bench, then leaned forward to touch his lips to her cheek. Softly. Reverently. "I was so afraid I'd never get the chance to tell you I love you. And that I'm sorry."

The flowing dress let her ease her knee onto the bench and turn to face him. She cupped his cheek and he kissed her palm. She ignored the tingle it caused and said what needed to be said. "We both made mistakes. It wasn't any one person's fault."

"No." He shook his head and she let her hand fall to cover his heart. "You did what you had to do," he said. "I guess I forgot what it's like to take orders. You were obligated to do as you were told and you still managed to do your duty while protecting Sam and me. I understand that now. If Dad had been as guilty as my brother pointed out he probably looked, no one would have believed we hadn't covered up for him. Especially with Sam on the task force. Please forgive a nitwit with a big mouth and a short temper."

What could she say? "Okay. As long as you forgive me for misjudging your father. You were right, too. It was too easy for me to believe he was guilty. I argued with the general that Max is a Christian, but I must not have really believed my position if I was so easily swayed to believe the worst."

"The point is that none of what happened matters to me," Travis told her. "I want you in my life. I'll do whatever I have to do to have you there. I'll work from wherever you're sent. I'll even play nice-nice with your commanding officers."

She couldn't help it. She laughed and thumped his chest. "No, you won't."

He ducked his head. "I'll try," he promised, then shrugged, a sheepish smile tipping his lips up at the corners even though he fought it. "And I'll probably fail, but I *will* try. And hard as it would be, I'll forget marriage if you still don't want to get married. I'll—"

"No," she interrupted, fingering a button on his jacket. "I don't want you to forget marriage. In fact, if the wife and babies plan you proposed when I was young and too insecure to accept is still an option, I'd like that. As long as a partnership in AdVance comes with the new name."

Travis's eyes went round with surprise. He opened his mouth. Closed it. Blinked. Then finally said, "Oh, it's an option. Except what about your career? You went through all you did for a promotion."

"It was mostly about protecting you almost from the beginning. And a promotion would probably take me to the Pentagon."

"D.C., huh?" He hesitated. "I can work out of D.C. I don't want you to give up your career for me."

He'd hate D.C. The traffic. The humidity. *She* hated D.C. "I wouldn't be giving up my career. I'd be changing it. For us." She shrugged. "Besides, it's already done. I turned down the promotion and I gave the general my resignation."

"When?" His eyes narrowed. "That's what you handed him?" He stabbed a hand through his hair. "But—"

"Trav! It's okay." She put her hands on his shoulders, willing him to believe her. "I've never had a family. I don't mean a husband and babies. I mean what you have right now. I not only don't want you to give that up, I want it, too. I want it for our children. For myself. The Air Force won't let me have that. The service was good for me and gave me the structure I'd never had and the purpose I needed. But I don't need either anymore. I need what I was afraid to reach out for before. I need you and the life we can have together."

He smiled and it was the most beautiful thing she'd ever seen. "Wow. I came out here to beg and *you* proposed to *me*."

"Travis," Max called out the back door, "everyone's gone. You can quit hiding out there."

"We're not hiding, Dad. Go away and quit interrupting. Tricia's in the middle of proposing," Travis called out.

Tricia felt her cheeks heat, and she swatted him, making him chuckle.

"Oh. Sorry, son. You aren't going to turn the girl down, are you? I'd hate to think I raised a fool for a son." The door closed with a thud.

"You are so bad!" she told him, laughing.

He tilted his head. "But you love me anyway," he told her.

She nodded and kissed him. "More than life itself," she told him.

"Yeah, I got that. The phone call tonight. It was about saving *me*, not *you*." He gazed at her as if afraid she might disappear in a puff of smoke. "I don't want to be pushy, but are we talking a long engagement here? Because I've waited an awfully long time for you already and I almost lost you tonight. November twentieth is a Saturday. I know it's only three weeks away—"

Her heart turned over in her chest. "You remember the day we met in college?" Who would have thought the grisly bear with the sore paw could morph into a teddy bear in the span of a month?

"Like it was yesterday." He chuckled. "My toe's still crooked from that book you dropped on it."

"I have a confession. I dropped it on purpose. I wanted to meet you but I didn't know how to just say hello. It wasn't supposed to hit you, let alone break your toe."

He chuckled. "I have a confession, too. I stuck my foot out. I wanted to meet you, too."

She laughed and took his hand. "Let's go tell your mother she has three weeks to plan a wedding."

* * * * *

Dear Reader,

I was so excited to be asked to join the FAITH ON THE LINE series for Love Inspired. My reason was pretty simple. I fear many of us, sitting in our safe little homes and going to our idyllic churches, forget that there are Christians out there in the line of fire. They go forth into danger, fighting the world's evils wherever they find them—for us. We need to remember that though many who don the mantle of warrior also wear the mantle of Jesus, they still need our continuous prayers. They face a double foe, the one they can see and another we all battle. Temptation is there all around them and they need our prayers to combat it.

I tried to show that battle as Travis lay in relative safety while taking aim at the men who would gleefully have killed the woman he loved if she were discovered. He prayed first for forgiveness as he contemplated his duty, but then he started feeling very righteous anger as they planned Tricia's death. Temptation had found its subtle inroad, and Travis felt the darkness engulfing him and he remembered to turn to God. Tricia also faced death, and she too steadfastly turned to her Lord for comfort. My prayer for all who wear uniforms and carry badges of authority is that they remember where to turn in those darkest of moments on the job and in the quiet aftermath.

I love hearing from readers at kate_welsh@earthlink.net, but I regret I can only answer e-mail correspondence, or letters accompanied with a self-addressed stamped envelope when you write through Love Inspired.

Love and blessings,

Kate Welsh

A long-lost Vance reappears in the jungles of
Venezuela to take down the leader of
La Mano Oscura—and reunites with his ex-wife,
in PETER'S RETURN,
coming only to Love Inspired
in November 2004.

And now for a sneak preview,
please turn the page.

Chapter One

She looked past him out the window and saw a sign for Santa Maria de Flores. "I think we're here."

They continued through the small primitive town, passing run-down houses and barefoot, half-clad children playing in the street. Emily frowned as the driver turned onto a small dirt road on the outskirts of town that led up into the hills. "Is this right? Shouldn't the clinic be back in the town?" Robert looked as nonplussed as she felt. She turned back to the driver. "Excuse me?" she said loudly.

"He probably doesn't understand English," Robert said.

"¿Con permiso?" she amended. Something was wrong with this driver. All joking aside, something really had been nagging her ever since she saw him in the airport holding up a Doctors Without Borders sign. Without question, they'd followed him like little lambs to the slaughter. "Con permiso," she said a little more forcefully, and this time tapped the driver's shoulder.

Ignoring her, the driver leaned forward and pushed

a button. Before she could take another breath, a clear partition rose between them. Emily looked into Robert's widened eyes. The shocked disbelief on his face would have been comical if it weren't for the sick feeling of dread growing in her stomach. "What are we going to do?" she whispered.

Robert tried to open his door, but it wouldn't budge. Then he tried the window. It, too, was immovable.

"Oh, Lord, protect us," Emily said between breaths that were suddenly coming too fast and too short.

"It's okay, don't panic. I've heard about these guys. If we pay them, they'll let us go. In fact, some are even desperate enough to take a check. Did you bring a checkbook?"

"Checkbook?" she blurted. "That's absurd. Who would I make it out to—Mr. Kidnapper?"

"It's true. I saw it on *20/20*."

"You're not serious?" Her eyes searched his. *He was.* "Let's pray it will be as simple as that," she muttered.

They didn't say another word as the driver took them deeper and deeper into the Venezuelan countryside.

Emily closed her eyes. She wanted to pray, but she couldn't bring herself to do it. It had been so long since she'd been able to connect with the Lord. She'd made a promise—not any ordinary promise, but a deathbed promise to God—and she'd broken it. She'd lived with the shame for so long it was almost automatic, almost comfortable. She couldn't go asking for more favors now.

Robert took her hand in his and she held it, thankful

for his warmth and friendship. She didn't know what she'd do if she were alone.

"We're going to be okay," he whispered. "You have to believe that."

She nodded. "I know. We have to be. We're doctors, we're the good guys. Not only that, we're Americans."

Robert smiled, and squeezed her hand before turning back toward the window as the driver veered off onto a gravel road. They were deep in the jungle now, not a sign of civilization in sight. Emily couldn't help wondering where they were being taken and under what kind of conditions they would be forced to live until their ransom was paid. *If* their ransom would be paid.

Don't think like that, she told herself, but the sad fact was she was alone in the world—no husband, no siblings, no family to come to her rescue. She swallowed her despair; she'd dealt with her parents' accident years ago, but Peter was another matter.

She lost touch with him and hadn't seen him—no one had—in a very long time. But if by some miracle of God he'd discovered she was gone, would he come looking for her? Would he care? The realization that she couldn't be sure brought little comfort, only the familiar squeeze of regret. His job, his mission, whatever it was he was working on always came before she did.

"Look!" Robert whispered, interrupting the well-worn path her thoughts were taking.

Emily sat up straighter as glimpses of a large stucco wall came into view. They turned a bend in the road then stopped before a tall iron gate. The driver nodded to the guard sitting in a booth and the gate swung open. Emily couldn't help but be riveted by the grounds inside the gates.

The parklike setting of benches and statues placed strategically beneath cascading trees surrounding a large duck-laden pond caught her breath. Tucked among the trees were several shrubs trimmed in various animal shapes. Flowers in every shape and size greeted them in a riot of color.

Here and there, she spotted the clay tile roofs of several small outbuildings. She tried to focus through the thick foliage, to get her bearings on the bungalows and see what their use was, but she could only catch scattered glimpses before they disappeared into the jungle. A golf cart passed, but instead of laughing tourists enjoying the eighteenth hole, two guards in tan uniforms with rifles slung over their shoulders watched the Suburban, giving their driver a slight nod as they passed.

They turned right onto a cobblestone road and slowly approached a breathtaking Spanish Colonial mansion. Emily leaned into Robert and whispered, "I don't think my checkbook is going to get us out of this one."

"Neither do I," he agreed, and a grim look of futility filled his face. She squeezed his hand as they followed the drive around back and parked in front of a garage larger than the elementary school on the corner of Emily's block back in Colorado Springs. In front of the garage, a series of golf carts were parked next to a bright-red Porsche.

"Pinch me, Robert. I think we've just been transported into a *Fantasy Island* rerun," she said, trying to lighten the mood.

"Shh, be serious and be quiet. Let me do all the talking."

"Gladly," she whispered. "And as soon as you get us out of this, I'll try not to remind you how sexist you are being."

"Deal," he grumbled. They watched the driver get out and open their door. "Just where are we?" Robert demanded with more bravado than Emily knew he felt.

"You are the guests of Mr. Escalante," the driver said, then stepped back and waited for them to get out of the car.

Robert stood, but didn't move out of the doorway, effectively blocking her exit. She pushed up on her knees and peeked around him. "I demand you take us to the Doctors Without Borders clinic," he insisted.

The driver tilted his chin down and gave Robert a bone-chilling stare. He gestured toward the mansion. "I suggest you cooperate. It will make your stay here a little more pleasant for all of us if you do." He stepped around Robert and held out his hand. "Dr. Armstrong."

Robert stepped aside. Without taking the driver's hand, Emily got out of the car. There was something dark and dangerous and almost slithering in the man's eyes. He looked like a man who wouldn't give a second's hesitation to killing them right there on the spot. This was not someone she wanted to touch.

The driver nodded, seeming to accept her slight and said, "Follow me."

Robert started forward and Emily followed close behind. "What do you think they want from us?" she said, leaning forward and whispering in his ear.

"I don't know," he said over his shoulder, "but whatever it is, cooperate."

"Of course I'll cooperate," she muttered. What made him think she wouldn't cooperate? As they walked through the lush grounds, Emily wondered if they could make a run for it. And if they did, how far would they get?

"Mr. Escalante's compound encompasses over two hundred acres," the driver said as they walked. "At all times, there are guards patrolling every inch of the estate in case you should ever need help."

That answered her question.

He gestured beyond the garages. "Through those trees is the tennis court and swimming pool. There is also a hot tub should you feel the desire to relax your muscles after your long journey."

Somehow she didn't think a hot tub would do the trick. As they walked, Emily tried not to be awed by the beauty of the plants, the orchids and the blooming vines hanging from trees. She sucked in a breath as she caught a glimpse of a red, blue and green macaw unlike she'd ever seen. "It's the Garden of Eden," she muttered.

"Yeah," Robert agreed. "But watch out for snakes."

The driver turned back and looked at them. The dead emptiness in his eyes curled her toes. "I hate snakes," she whispered, and tried to smother the prickling sensation moving through her.

The man led them into a walled-in, shaded courtyard

complete with a mosaic of Spanish tiles and a large fountain. Robert stopped next to an intricate wrought-iron table. "Why have you brought us here?" he demanded, and refused to take another step.

The driver kept walking.

Emily threw Robert a pointed look. "What should we call you?" she asked in her most pleasant and professional voice that barely hid the anxiousness squeezing her throat.

The man halted and turned back, his cold, predatory gaze stopping her in her tracks. "Snake."

Take 2 inspirational love stories FREE!

PLUS get a FREE surprise gift!

Mail to Steeple Hill Reader Service™

In U.S.	In Canada
3010 Walden Ave.	P.O. Box 609
P.O. Box 1867	Fort Erie, Ontario
Buffalo, NY 14240-1867	L2A 5X3

YES! Please send me 2 free Love Inspired® novels and my free surprise gift. After receiving them, if I don't wish to receive anymore, I can return the shipping statement marked cancel. If I don't cancel, I will receive 4 brand-new novels every month, before they're available in stores! Bill me at the low price of $4.24 each in the U.S. and $4.74 each in Canada, plus 25¢ shipping and handling and applicable sales tax, if any*. That's the complete price and a savings of over 10% off the cover prices—quite a bargain! I understand that accepting the books and gift places me under no obligation ever to buy any books. I can always return a shipment and cancel at any time. Even if I never buy another book from Steeple Hill, the 2 free books and the surprise gift are mine to keep forever.

113 IDN DZ9M
313 IDN DZ9N

Name	(PLEASE PRINT)	
Address	Apt. No.	
City	State/Prov.	Zip/Postal Code

Not valid to current Love Inspired® subscribers.

Want to try two free books from another series?
Call 1-800-873-8635 or visit www.morefreebooks.com.

* Terms and prices are subject to change without notice. Sales tax applicable in New York. Canadian residents will be charged applicable provincial taxes and GST. All orders subject to approval. Offer limited to one per household.

® are registered trademarks owned and used by the trademark owner and or its licensee.

INTLI04R   ©2004 Steeple Hill

DELILAH AND STEEPLE HILL BOOKS
WANT TO REWARD YOU THIS FALL WITH THE GIFT OF SONG

This October and November when you purchase two Love Inspired® books, you'll receive Delilah's Love Songs CD (a retail value of approximately $15.00 U.S.).

Name (PLEASE PRINT)

Address   Apt. #

City   State/Prov.   Zip/Postal Code

To receive your DELILAH LOVE SONGS CD complete the above form. Mail it to the address below with 2 proof of purchase tokens (found in the back of all October and November 2004 Love Inspired® books). Requests containing Proof of Purchase tokens must be postmarked no later than December 5, 2004. Please allow 30-60 days for delivery. Offer valid in the U.S. only, while quantities last. Offer limited to one per household.

Steeple Hill/Delilah
c/o P.O. Box 5097
Rockefeller Center Station
New York, NY 10185

Steeple
Hill®

Visit us at www.radiodelilah.com
and www.SteepleHill.com

LIDPROMO